DAUGHTERS *of the* SEA

Hannah

KATHRYN LASKY

DAUGHTERS *of the* SEA

Hannah

SCHOLASTIC PRESS / NEW YORK

Library of Congress Cataloging-in-Publication Data

Lasky, Kathryn.
Daughters of the sea : Hannah / by Kathryn Lasky.
p. cm.
Summary: In 1899 when a fifteen-year-old orphan named Hannah obtains
employment as a servant in the home of one of Boston's wealthiest
families, she meets a noted portrait painter who seems to know things
about her that even she is not aware of, and when she accompanies
the family to their summer home in Maine, she feels an undeniable pull
to the sea.
ISBN-13: 978-0-439-78310-1 (alk. paper)
ISBN-10: 0-439-78310-0 (alk. paper)
[1. Mermaids—Fiction. 2. Identity—Fiction. 3. Social classes—Fiction.
4. Household employees—Fiction. 5. Orphans—Fiction. 6. Boston
(Mass.)—History—1865—Fiction. 7. Maine—History—
19th century—Fiction.] I. Title. II. Title: Hannah.
PZ7.L3274Da 2009
[Fic]—dc22
2009008433
10 9 8 7 6 5 4 3 2 1   09 10 11 12 13
Printed in the U.S.A.   23
First edition, September 2009

The text type was set in ITC Cheltenham Book.
Book design by Lillie Mear

Full fathom five thy father lies;
Of his bones are coral made;
Those are pearls that were his eyes:
Nothing of him that doth fade,
But doth suffer a sea-change
Into something rich and strange.
Sea-nymphs hourly ring his knell.

—William Shakespeare,
The Tempest

A PORT CITY

THEY SAY THE SEA makes some people sick. Its slow, billowing waves swelling beneath a ship make stomachs heave. But for Hannah Albury, this was unimaginable. It was land that made her sick. Sick near to dying.

She would have never left the sea had it not been for Miss Pringle at the orphanage — The Boston Home for Little Wanderers. How she detested that woman, with her thin, piercing voice that reminded Hannah of a needle.

The sickness started with Go Forth Day. *Go Forth* was the name that The Home for Little Wanderers called the day when girls who had reached their fourteenth year learned where they were to be sent. It was a day halfway between a graduation and an eviction.

The girls were considered too old to continue living off the charity of others and had to start earning their keep in the world. That day had arrived a year before for Hannah and a dozen other girls, but a scarlet fever epidemic had postponed it, giving them a reprieve. Now the scarlet fever was long gone, and it was time for them to leave.

The girls had all passed their fifteenth birthdays and sat waiting with this year's fourteen-year-olds to be called, one by one, into Miss Pringle's office and learn their destinies.

They sat in alphabetical order in a row of chairs. There were two *A*s who came before Hannah: Lucy Abbott and Tilly Adams. The girls waited, whispering in excited voices to one another. Except for Hannah, who sat locked in silence.

Until this moment, the girls had indulged in a range of fantasies about who they really were, how some grievous mistake or cruel twist of fate had caused them, quite by accident, to become orphans. In their own minds, they had been products of wealthy, stylish families. Perhaps even royal families, as Sadie Crawford persisted in believing. Sadie was convinced that her own mother was a princess from France, or sometimes Russia. When the girls went forth, they imagined that some of these errors would be redressed.

"Just wait and see, Bessie," said Sadie, who sat next to Hannah in alphabetical order. "If I get sent up to one of those fine homes on Commonwealth Avenue, they will surely see that I have refinements most uncommon. And if they have a son, he might fall in love with me and then I can seek out my true mother because he will have enough money to help me find her —"

"Do you remember Martha Gilmore, Sadie?" Bessie responded, lost in her own inventions. "Well, Martha, she got a job in a hat shop down on Washington Street, and one day, the day she turned eighteen, actually, a man came in to buy a hat for his wife, and guess what?"

"What?" Sadie said.

"He fell in love with her and he divorced his wife and married her. Martha was so lovely and refined that he couldn't help himself. He saw that she was much more than a mere salesgirl."

"Divorce?" Sadie gasped. "Oh, I wouldn't want anything like that — royalty doesn't divorce." Sadie turned to Hannah. "Don't you agree, Hannah?"

There was a burst of giggles down the row of chairs.

"Why would you ask Hannah?" someone whispered.

Why indeed? Hannah thought. Hannah was not one to indulge in the favorite pastime of the girls at the home. These reveries of alternate lives fed the girls, nourished them, gave them hope. Hannah was not inclined toward dreams.

Lucy Abbott had just come out of Miss Pringle's office. She was glowing.

"Where are you to go?" A very tiny girl, Cornelia Ellis, jumped up.

"There's an opening for a scullery girl at that fancy gentlemen's restaurant on Winter Street. If I do well, I might be able to work at the hatcheck desk. You know, where the men leave off their hats and coats."

"Hats! Hats! That's the answer!" Bessie exclaimed. "What did I tell you about Martha Gilmore! Oh, you're on your way, Lucy! You always said you thought your father was a true Bostonian!"

"Yes, yes, high born, I think. Maybe a wool mer-chant." Lucy nodded.

"What better place to meet him than that fancy restaurant?"

Hannah settled back in her chair. She had no such thoughts, no such dreams of her parents. High born, low born, or anything else. It all seemed out of the realm of possibility that she had connections to any-one. She couldn't even imagine what to hope for in terms of her placement, and she felt her heart sink a bit as she watched Tilly Adams walk through Miss Pringle's office door. She would be next. Did it really matter where she might go?

But not ten minutes later, Hannah stood before Miss Pringle in stunned silence and marveled at how she could have ever been stupid enough to think that it wasn't important.

"Rules are rules." Miss Pringle sat erect behind her desk and sorted some papers that evidently pertained to Hannah. "The board of directors of the home has a policy about children who, upon reaching the age of fourteen, seem unsuitable for domestic employment — and that you are unsuitable, have no doubts, Hannah. I could no more send you into the home of a Boston family of society" — she pronounced the word "so-sigh-it-tee," so each syllable had a poisonous little ping to it — "than teach a cow how to fly!"

"But what about a position in a shop or —"

"Don't interrupt. And, no, you are no more suitable for a shop than a position in a home."

"Why not?" Hannah burst out.

Miss Pringle's mouth settled into a firm line and she regarded Hannah with a look that seemed to say *Where should I begin?*

"I can read and write better than a lot of the girls here." Hannah tried to keep her voice firm as her world reeled.

"So, I suppose, you think that you should be a stenographer or a social secretary?"

"Maybe." Hannah spoke softly, barely concealing her defiance.

"No 'maybe' about it. Definitely not! For one thing you would have to be older for such a job. And despite your writing skills, you are generally rather awkward. We can't have you going into a Boston home and spilling their dinners and breaking their Wedgwood." Hannah had no idea what Wedgwood was, but she hadn't spilled things *that* often. "So there will be no more of this talk. The board says that a child for whom placement cannot be found in Boston must be put on an orphan train."

"But I thought the whole point was that now that I am fifteen, I am too old to be considered an orphan? That is why the home is putting me out. So how can I be put on an orphan train?" Hannah was pleased with the logic of her argument. Miss Pringle was not.

Her eyes drilled into Hannah. "You see, Hannah," she barked. "That is precisely the problem. You know no boundaries. You argue, you challenge. Now, how can I send someone like you into a fine home or a decent shop?"

"But I'm not an orphan now. I'm too old."

"Not in Kansas you aren't," Miss Pringle said matter-of-factly and stood up to signal that the interview had ended. "The next shipment is to depart within a week for Salina, Kansas."

"Shipment?" Hannah said weakly.

"Yes, shipment of orphans."

"Is anyone else from the home supposed to go? Will there be others?"

"No. We found suitable placements for them."

Suitable. Why was she considered so unsuitable? She hated the word. It was not the first time she had heard it. Miss Pringle used it the most, but the other adults at the home had picked up on it. The domestic arts teacher, Miss Baker, had just said it the other day when Hannah had gone to comfort a newly arrived orphan girl with a fresh warm bun from the kitchen.

"You can't just barge into the kitchen and take things without asking. That's most unsuitable, Hannah!"

"Why? She's hungry," Hannah had replied.

"To question your elders is also unsuitable," Miss Eakins, the home's nurse, who happened to be walking by, had chimed in.

But Hannah now merely took a deep breath and asked Miss Pringle another question. "Is Kansas near the sea, ma'am?"

"Heavens, no! I took you for being brighter than that, child!" Miss Pringle glared at her, then in an acid voice said, "Certainly, not so bright as to match the brightness of your hair!"

The sun streaming through the window had ignited the red highlights of the unpinned hair that tumbled over Hannah's shoulders like a cataract of flames. It was a peculiarity of her hair that the color changed with the light. On cloudy days drizzling with rain, it appeared dull, a guttering flame wrapped in fog. On a brilliant winter day with the sun reflecting off snow and glistening icicles, her hair was as dazzling as rubies. And if she were near the sea toward dawn or dusk in a gathering of shadows, her hair acquired a slightly greenish cast, like old copper.

In two quick steps, Miss Pringle strode to a bookshelf and fetched an atlas. Opening it to a map of the United States, she stuck her ink-stained index finger on a spot in the middle and tapped it several times, then snickered. "It's about as far from any sea as you could get."

That was when Hannah felt the first strange twinge of the sickness.

A LOVELY CHILD?

A WEEK LATER Hannah was aboard the train. She spent her first morning observing her fellow orphan travelers. Some appeared to be her age or older, but these were in the minority. Most were much younger, under ten years old. She wondered if the few who were her age had somehow failed to "go forth" as she had. Several of these young people had boarded the train in New York. Perhaps they, like herself, were deemed unfit to serve as domestics in the grand houses of that city.

She did not hear any fanciful tales, as she had in Boston, of orphan fates twisted away from their true destinies of distinguished families with great fortune. And yet she could not help but notice that all of the children seemed excited, full of anticipation. One particularly dingy little girl whose skin looked as if it had never seen the light of day spoke with great animation about the "wide country."

"I hear that there is at least a mile between every house and sometimes more. That's why they need children to fill up the land."

"And to work," said another girl. "They got more cows and chickens out there than people."

"The work's not that hard and there is lots of time to play outside. Meadows for picnics and all," said a plump girl with a band of freckles across her nose.

"Do you know how to milk a cow?" asked another.

"No, but I reckon I can learn fast enough. It can't be that hard."

"Maybe we'll all end up being farmers' wives." This caused a great uproar.

"Hey, you!" A girl with curly black hair and bright blue eyes addressed Hannah, who was sitting across the aisle. "You want to be a farmer's wife?"

"Oh, Maisy!" Her seatmate giggled.

"I don't think I'm old enough to be anybody's wife. Farmer or not." Hannah laughed softly in reply to Maisy.

"Oh, they marry young," Maisy said. "You just wait. Why, you look old enough to me. How old are you?"

"Fifteen," Hannah replied.

"A girl at our orphanage ran off with the milkman when she was fourteen," Maisy went on. "And you're much prettier than she is."

"Thank you," Hannah replied.

"And I bet you're smarter, too. I saw you reading that newspaper that you found on the floor. See, if you were a farmer's wife, you could keep track of the crops — write them all down and the price. You do figures?"

"Yes, even a little bit of long division," Hannah added.

"Well, there you go! You really could be a farmer's wife, keep all the accounts. I knew you were different the first time I clapped eyes on you when I got on in New York. I said to my best friend, Amy, here, 'Look at her. Ain't she a different-looking thing?'" Hannah was not sure how to respond. It was not as if Maisy was making fun of her, not in the least. There was only kindness in Maisy's remarks.

"But me," freckle-faced Polly began, "I think I'd rather be a farmer's daughter than a wife, because if your father, say, owned a huge cattle ranch, then you'd maybe get a cowboy for a boyfriend. They have big ranches out West and handsome cowboys."

A bright light suffused Polly's face and soon a hush fell on the others. All the girls were beginning to construct their Western dreams, their fantasy lives. They were no different from the girls back at The Home for Little Wanderers. And they all felt that this train was carrying them toward something. But Hannah felt she was moving away, farther and farther with each mile that the train devoured the track. It was also right then that the twinges she had first felt in Miss Pringle's office turned into pain.

Later that same night, somewhere between Pennsylvania and Ohio, Polly looked down at Hannah's wrists and asked, "What's that?" Tiny, dark red bumps had appeared where the cuffs of Hannah's dress ended. By noon the bumps had spread to her hands and were creeping up her neck.

One of the matrons who was in charge of the children took Hannah into a private compartment and made her take off all her clothes. Her body was a conflagration. The woman inhaled sharply.

"You say you've had measles?"

"Yes, ma'am."

"Well, that's a relief, we don't want to be bringing a plague to the middle of the country." Hannah felt a shock course through her entire body. A double shock that she could be the source of a plague and then those awful words "middle of the country."

"What other symptoms have you had?"

"Symptoms?" Hannah wasn't sure what the woman meant.

"You know — itching."

Until the woman mentioned it Hannah hadn't itched, but suddenly she did. It was the worst in the regions that her combis — her sewn-together chemise and drawers — covered. "I think that if I could take my combis off, it would help."

"You mean travel without your underwear?" The woman's eyes widened. She was completely speechless for several seconds. "You mean naked? Are you depraved, child?"

"No, I'm just itchy. It's only the clothes beneath my dress. I won't be naked. No one will know."

"But . . . but . . . I'll know," the matron sputtered.

"But you won't tell . . . I mean, what does it matter?"

The matron's mouth quivered, and then her thin lips pleated with vertical lines moved, but no sound was forthcoming. It was as if they were feeling their way around the shape of words she could not quite utter.

"I won't tell anyone," Hannah said. "Not a soul."

Finally the matron spoke. "No, you shan't." Hannah felt a little worm of panic squirm deep in her gut. "You shall remain in here. In this compartment for the rest of the trip."

"But it's so tiny!"

The matron continued to stare at Hannah, saying nothing.

"And what if I have to . . . you know, go to the privy?" Hannah asked.

"I'll bring you a pot."

"But I don't understand! I won't be able to talk to any of the others. Why are you punishing me? I'll wear my combis and itch. I don't want to be alone."

"You are infected!"

No, I'm not! Hannah wanted to scream. But she could feel her own skin drying up and suddenly yearned for the fog-drenched air of Boston, the moist winds coming off the water.

"You better pray this rash doesn't spread to your face," the matron snapped. "No one will ever want to adopt you then!" The woman turned and shut the door.

The window in the compartment was much smaller than the one in the passenger section, but it didn't matter. Hannah didn't need to look out to feel that she was getting farther and farther away from the ocean.

Matron would come by and set down a tin bowl of food, but Hannah rarely touched it. She had no appetite. Time ceased to have meaning for her. Although the itching was always present, it was as if there were times when she left her own body, slipped the prickly inferno of her skin, and entered a kind of dream state. With extreme concentration, she could conjure up the feel of the sea wind against her skin.

It was very late one night when the train pulled into a tiny station somewhere out in the middle of the empty plains, and the conductor called out, "Enterprise! Next stop — Salina."

Hannah knew that she had better get dressed but the very idea of wearing the combis made her itch horribly. She decided to leave them off. When she got up to reach for her other clothes, she noticed that the floor near the pallet and the pallet itself were covered with what looked like sparkling white dust. However, when she stooped down to examine it more closely, she noticed that it was actually small crystals of what appeared to be sugar. *But did they come from me?* she wondered.

Impulsively Hannah scraped up some of the crystals in her palm and then stuck out the tip of her tongue. *Salt!* Not sugar at all, but definitely salt. How odd! Immediately she noticed a cool vapor on her tongue, accompanied by a tingling sensation. It felt as if the salt crystals were dissolving but leaving some kind of residue. She stuck out her tongue tip again and picked off a tiny chip. She blinked. On the tip of her finger rested a flat, nearly oval sliver that seemed almost to glow with iridescence.

A welter of emotions coursed through Hannah. She was intrigued and confused, then nearly overcome with a sudden deep and dreadful shame. Had these strange salt crystals really come from *her*? She felt compelled to get rid of this . . . this evidence of her own freakishness. She began sweeping them up in her hands as fast as she could, before the matron came in. She looked around for a refuse bin. But just as she was about to throw them away, she stopped. Her hand froze. She felt something surge up inside her. She closed her hand around the crystals she had gathered and thrust them into her pocket.

By the time the train reached Salina, Hannah's face had swollen to twice its normal size. A woman of considerable bulk approached her with the matron. "What have we here?" She looked down at Hannah, peering through her pince-nez-style spectacles embedded in a fold of fat that seemed provided especially for the task of holding them.

"She has a rash, Mrs. Phillips. I don't think it's any cause for concern. She's a lovely child."

Hannah shot the matron a furious look. *So lovely that you stuck me in a tiny horrid compartment and half the time you forgot to take my privy pot to empty.*

"Just a reaction," the matron continued. "An allergic reaction." She spoke nervously.

"A reaction to what?" Mrs. Phillips asked.

"My combis," Hanna said quickly. "I'm naked under this dress. Naked as a jaybird," she said pointedly and looked at matron.

"Oh, my! She'll have to be broken!" Mrs. Phillips said and smiled. "Well, dear, we're the rodeo capital of Kansas. Bronco busting is our *spécialité*." She pronounced the word in a foreign-sounding way.

"You're going to break me . . . break me in half?"

"Oh, no, dear," Mrs. Phillips said with a warm chuckle and took Hannah's red hand. Hannah saw matron wince. "Breaking is just an expression. It means putting a saddle on a wild thing so it can be ridden."

Hannah shut her eyes. She wasn't going to ask anything else.

"What's her name?" Mrs. Phillips asked matron.

"Let me see a minute. I have it right here." She had been holding a piece of paper. "Uh . . . uh . . . you're not Loretta."

"Hannah. I'm Hannah Albury," she said quietly.

"All right, Hannah Albury, follow me." Much to matron's horror, Mrs. Phillips took Hannah by the hand and led her firmly away, apparently not worried about being infected.

In addition to the lack of underwear, the red rash, and her swollen face, Hannah was also emaciated. With every mile that had taken her away from the old port city of Boston and the sea, Hannah's queasiness had increased. She had eaten very little and by the time the train had reached the eastern edge of the great prairie states, with those undulating fields of wheat and corn, she could not keep even the slightest morsel of food in her stomach.

A quarter of an hour after arriving in Salina, Hannah stood along with fifty other girls and boys, most of them from an orphanage in New York, on a raised platform in the town hall. Mr. Benedict, one of the agents from the New York Children's Aid Society, announced the names of the applicant families, who then proceeded to come onto the platform and select a child to take back to their farms. Strong twelve-year-old boys were the first to be chosen, followed closely by chubby, irresistible girl toddlers. Polly was the exception. She was the second child picked. Though pudgy and not exactly an obvious choice for farmwork, she was adorable with her dimples and what matron called her lovely quiet ways. Hannah smirked and wanted to call out, "She said I was lovely, too."

Instead, she watched as couples left with their new "sons" and "daughters." She studied the faces of the people remaining and wondered if any one of them would see beyond her swollen red face to something else that might make them want her. But she also didn't want to be wanted — maybe if no one wanted her, they would send her back. She kept her hand deep in the pocket of her dress and felt the little glistening crystals. For some reason she found it calming to touch them.

Just as this notion of being sent back kindled a spark of hope within her, she saw two tall, skinny elderly people standing in front of her with Mr. Benedict. The man wore a preacher's white collar. "We'll take the poor thing. For a spell," the woman said. "We're Christians, after all."

Whatever spark had been kindled was suddenly extinguished. Hannah was not being rejected — not totally, at least. Nor was she being accepted. She was to be tolerated for a spell. She was what was left when the bottom of the orphan barrel was scraped, an object of Christian charity.

The Stubbses were nice enough. However, as soon as Hannah set foot in their house, which perched on a hillock at the edge of town, her health began to fail even more precipitously. The crystals created a tiny blizzard every time she got up from the bed in the small room off the parlor that she was given to sleep in. She tried to be careful and collect them, but it wasn't long before Mrs. Stubbs found them.

"What's this?"

"It's me. I don't know why. I think the air is too dry or something."

Dr. Rose from town was called immediately. He was solicitous and gentle as he examined her.

He balanced one of the crystals on the tip of his finger. "I've never seen anything quite like it. It appears at first glance like dermatitis. Yet the structure is so odd, the shape, not flat, but . . . but . . ." He paused a long time. He never appeared to finish the thought and instead turned toward the Stubbses. "Reverend, do you perhaps have a magnifying glass so that I could examine these more carefully?"

Reverend Stubbs returned from his study with the magnifying glass. "Curious . . . very curious. I haven't ever seen anything like this." Hannah felt a terrible fear well up in her as she watched the doctor squinting through the magnifying glass at her crystals. It seemed like an awful transgression, an invasion of not just her privacy but her being.

The doctor looked up and peered now at Hannah. "Where do you come from?"

"Boston," Hannah whispered. He blinked as if the answer was somehow slightly unsatisfactory.

"I mean . . ." He hesitated. "Your parents, do you know anything about them?"

"She's an orphan, Doctor. Came on the orphan train," Gertrude Stubbs replied and gave a shrug. But the doctor was not paying attention to her. His gaze was fixed on Hannah.

"Their nationality, child . . . Irish perhaps? Lots of Irish in Boston, and you with that red hair."

Now it was Hannah's turn to shrug. "Sorry," she replied softly. "I don't know anything about them."

"You were collected then as an infant?"

Collected seemed an odd word but she guessed that was how it had been. "Yes."

"No early memories of anything?"

Hannah had never really thought about early memories. She'd been an orphan since birth. But as she concentrated, intimate, familiar feelings began to stir in Hannah. Like the cool mist she had first felt on her tongue when she tasted the salt crystal, these feelings rose within her, tiny vaporous droplets meandering, dancing slowly in a circle. And with these stirrings came a longing for some *thing*, a yearning. How could she yearn for something she did not know?

"Reverend." The doctor turned to the Stubbses. "Might I trouble you for an envelope? I would like to take some of these . . . these . . ." He searched for a word. "Crystals with me as specimens. I am catching the noon train today to attend a medical conference in Kansas City and would like to discuss this . . . this condition with my colleagues, and perhaps take a closer look at the specimens through a microscope."

Hannah suddenly forgot her itching as panic welled up within her. She did not like being referred to as a "specimen," but even more she did not like the idea of half a dozen doctors peering through microscopes at her crystals. If there was a secret about her, it was hers to know, to discover. Not the doctor's. She had to stop what was about to happen.

"Certainly," the reverend replied.

Gertrude Stubbs invited the doctor to have a cup of coffee and her homemade apple tart.

"Can't pass that up!" the doctor replied.

When the reverend came back with the envelope, the doctor picked up the tweezers and carefully plucked some of the crystals that had drifted onto the blanket. He turned to Hannah and asked, "Might I take one of these crystals from your feet? Mrs. Stubbs says that it is your feet that cause you the most trouble."

Hannah's mind was working furiously. She couldn't say no.

"Don't worry. It won't hurt," the doctor added.

But when he uncovered her feet and he plucked what appeared to be a crystal from between her toes, she felt a stabbing pain.

"Oh. I am sorry, dear." He was clearly flustered. "Well, I think I have enough." He took the envelope and placed it in the open leather bag with his stethoscope and other instruments and then followed the Stubbses into their kitchen.

The moment he was out of sight, Hannah slipped from her bed and went into the reverend's study. On his desk was the sermon he had been working on for next Sunday's church service. It didn't take her long to find an envelope identical to the one he had given the doctor. She slipped the empty envelope into the leather bag in place of the one with the crystals. He had tucked in the flap, and she doubted he would open it until he was at the medical conference.

That afternoon Hannah took a turn for the worse. She felt parched, as if she were breaking into little pieces, losing herself bit by bit, and she lay feverish in her bed. Mrs. Stubbs had left the door open so Hannah could call to her if she needed anything. But Hannah knew that all she needed was to get away. Outside she could hear the whine of the wind across the prairie. The sound was dry and sibilant. So different from the blustery gusts off Boston harbor.

A visitor had come to discuss church activities, and Hannah could hear her talking with Mrs. Stubbs. The subject was not the wedding and baptism that would be occurring on the same weekend. Nor was it the new embroidered altar cloth that had provoked much discussion because of its bright colors and elaborate design. Rather they were speaking of Hannah.

"Doc Rose left for Kansas City and she took a turn for the worse. There's that new young doctor over in Pilcher but I think there is something very peculiar afflicting this child. I mean Doc Rose took some of her skin specimens with him."

"Skin specimens! My word!" Elisabeth Blanchard exclaimed. "What are you talking about, Gert?"

"I didn't tell you about the skin?"

"No, you didn't. Just a rash you said."

"Oh, no, much worse. There's something very strange about the child. These sparkly tiny bits that look like sugar or salt, she sheds them. Doc called them crystals. Like a blizzard. I tell you, Elisabeth, I spend half my day sweeping up after her. I swear the child has more layers than an onion. I mean, Lord knows — oh, pardon me — but I'm desperate. Lord knows what she'll look like when she's finished peeling away. She's a fright as it is. Enough to scare the black off a crow!" Her voice dropped. "I'm scared that she might die on us."

It was as if she were blaming Hannah for having the nerve to die, when they might be held responsible.

"What does Doc Rose say about this condition of hers?"

The reverend came into the room and interjected, "He says it's strange. 'Outlandish!' he called it."

"Oh, he's always with those big dramatic words," Elisabeth Blanchard said.

But to Hannah the word did not seem dramatic or big or complicated at all. It seemed accurate. That night she grew even sicker and sweated so mightily that the sheets were not just damp but wringing wet. She smelled salt, and when she somehow propped herself up, she saw that where her head had rested there was a glistening imprint — like the rime of frost on a windowpane. Only it wasn't frost, it was salt. She lifted the top sheet and gasped as she saw that her arms had left a similar salty imprint. Weakly, she climbed out of the bed and pulled the blankets all the way back. It was as if a salt ghost had slept in the bed.

Outside, the wind was blowing, blowing hard. In her bare feet Hannah managed to walk over to the window in the parlor. She felt not exactly weak, but so light it was as if she had no weight, as if she had dissolved and were no longer flesh and bone, but something almost vaporous. A small rolling fog bank. She drifted through the darkness of the house to a window that faced east, and gazed out longingly.

Hannah had heard talk on the train that Kansas was known for its terrible tornadoes that started in the spring. She listened while some described unimaginably enormous funnel clouds that spun wrathfully across the prairies, sucking up anything in their path. Houses, buggies, entire buildings. There was even a story about a freight train being ripped from the tracks and flung into a town several miles away, where it landed on top of the town's train depot and smashed it to bits. Hannah looked out the parlor window, scanning the horizon that now appeared purple against the blackness of the sky for a funnel cloud. If a tornado could pick up a train and fling it several miles, couldn't it suck her up and spit her out back east?

She was so absorbed in her thoughts that she hadn't heard the creak of the Stubbses' feet on the floor as they walked into the parlor, holding their bedside candle. They were stunned when they saw Hannah standing by the window. She looked like a silvery specter in the night, no more substantial than the tumbleweed that whirled across their yard. She seemed to float rather than stand, and her skin appeared almost translucent. Her eyes were luminous and her red hair fell in rippling cascades to her waist. So peculiar, so "outlandish" did she appear that Gertrude Stubbs went limp and sagged against her husband. But her husband's eyes were fixed on the glittering crystals that had been silvered by the moonlight streaming in through the window. They seemed to blow about Hannah's feet like a radiant mist. He thought at first it was the moonlight that infused the crystals with the vibrant hues, but when he looked closer he saw colors he had never seen in the moon's path — soft iridescent hues of lavender and gold, twinkling shades of rose and green that matched the strange green highlights that he suddenly noticed in her hair. Was she real? A shade? A spirit? Had she just died and left this shimmering dust in her wake as she passed out of this world to the next?

"Child?" The Reverend Stubbs took a step closer while his wife clung to him as a drowning person would to a scrap of wood in a storm-torn sea. "Child," he repeated. "What are you doing here by the window?"

Praying for a tornado! Hannah was tempted to say. *Praying for anything to get me back.* Finally she simply said the truth, "I have to go back East, back to Boston. I'll die here if I don't."

Gertrude Stubbs seemed to straighten up a bit. She leaned toward Hannah. "You really think so, child?"

"I know so," Hannah replied. "I have prayed to God every night. I must go back. This land is not good for me. It would be a blessing for me to return to Boston."

"A blessing?" The reverend and his wife both whispered the word and looked at each other. Who were they to deny a blessing to one of God's creatures, strange though she may be? The reverend cut off the thought as he looked down at the iridescent crystals that now seemed to him like a pathway pointing east. "Yes, you must go back," he said forcefully. "You must."

And so it was arranged that Hannah would return on the next eastbound train. The very thought of it seemed to initiate a miraculous restoration. Her appetite improved. She was able to keep down simple foods and the rash began to disappear.

The board of The Boston Home for Little Wanderers had declared that she was too old to remain there in the orphanage. And Miss Pringle had said in no uncertain terms that she was not suitable for domestic service. But Hannah knew she would have to find something that she was suitable for. Of one thing she was certain. She had to return to the sea.

"THEY ALL FIT"

HANNAH LOOKED OUT onto Boston Harbor at the steamer and the stevedores unloading the cargo. There was precious little difference between herself and burlap bags of coffee beans, she thought, both commodities for trading. If spoiled, they were dumped or burned. An inspector on board the ship walked down the gangplank, now nodding to the shipping agent that all had been received in good order. Anything contaminated would not have been permitted to off-load at this pier but would have been taken by a garbage tug to be sunk at sea or destroyed on "trash island," which was obscured by a thick veil of oily, dark smoke.

When Hannah had arrived back at the home, she was delighted to find that Miss Pringle had been replaced by a gentler woman, a Mrs. Larkin. Mrs. Larkin was younger, prettier, and possessed of a soft, lovely voice that was nothing like a needle but more like water bubbling in a lively stream.

"I don't see why you would be unsuitable for domestic service, my dear. Perhaps not upstairs serving tea immediately, but certainly you could help in the kitchen. Can you sew, Hannah?"

"Yes, ma'am."

"Well, there you go!" she said cheerfully.

Then Mrs. Larkin opened a folder and raised a finger, declaring, "Aha! The Hawleys. Mr. and Mrs. Horace Hawley, number Eighteen Louisburg Square, three daughters, ages nine to sixteen." She looked up with a merry light in her hazel eyes. "Oh my goodness, if they are anything like my sisters and me, their clothing will need constant attention and repair. I think this is just the place for you."

"Louisburg Square? That's in Boston, isn't it?" Hannah asked.

"Yes, my dear. Beacon Hill, one of the finest addresses in the city. The Hawleys are very . . ." She searched for a word. "Well, very refined, a very old Boston family and very wealthy." Then she hastened to add, "But don't let that worry you. You won't be serving at parties, as I said. You'll be . . . well, more or less in the shadows." Mrs. Larkin now leaned forward. "But it will be a comfortable setting and earn you almost one hundred dollars a year."

"One hundred dollars!" Hannah gasped. This was an unimaginable sum. Hannah had never had in her possession a single dollar before, had never felt in her hand the crumpled sturdiness of a bill.

"The starting wage for a scullery girl is one dollar and seventy-five cents per week. You get room and board, and you work seven days a week, but get two Sundays off a month."

"Starting wage," Hannah whispered.

"Yes, starting wage." Mrs. Larkin cocked her head to one side and regarded Hannah carefully. "But that is just starting. Do a good job and you can work your way up. The head upstairs maid makes over five hundred dollars a year and the cook . . . oh my goodness, cooks and butlers make almost a thousand dollars a year. I know you are bright and you will do well at the Hawleys'."

"You mean . . ." Hannah hesitated. She could not find the words as real hope sprung up in her. "You . . . think I am suitable?"

"Yes, dear. Now, here's the address and I am not sure if you will be speaking with Mrs. Hawley directly. It might be the butler or the head housekeeper, or perhaps the cook, but just be sweet. Don't ask too many questions. I shall send a letter along that says you can read. And do you do any figures, dear?"

"I can do sums and know my multiplication tables, and I was beginning to learn long division."

"Wonderful — almost fit for Harvard!"

"What's Harvard, ma'am?"

And now Mrs. Larkin laughed very hard. "Oh, you don't need to know about Harvard, dear. They don't admit girls." Hannah bit her lip lightly while she thought. She was determined to do well in this job, learn everything she could. It wasn't just the money, the promise of higher wages. It was the chance to live within reach of the sea. The salt crystals had stopped forming on her skin, but the crystals in the envelope that she had brought back seemed to have intensified in their color. She kept them now in a little pouch that she wore around her neck, tucked discreetly inside her camisole. Like a charm, a talisman she seemed to need to keep close to her.

"Hannah," Mrs. Larkin said loudly, calling her back from her reveries. "Is there anything else?"

"No . . . but it's a lot of money one could make someday, isn't it?"

"Indeed! And what would you do with more money?"

Hannah cocked her head. She had never thought about such a question until this moment. But then it came to her — a stunning realization and yet so obvious. "Why, I'd buy a house. Well, not a house — a little cottage by the sea."

Mrs. Larkin pulled her chin in and tipped her head back as if to take in a fuller measure of Hannah. "Hannah, you're . . . you're very original."

And now Hannah grew very quiet. "No . . . not really, I just know where I am comfortable, where I belong. And that is near the sea."

"Any sea?" Mrs. Larkin asked.

"Is there more than one?" Hannah replied.

"Oh, yes, my dear! But the Atlantic Ocean is closest to us."

"That will do," Hannah said simply.

Mrs. Larkin looked at Hannah curiously, and then she laughed. "Well, I'm glad. I would hate for you to have to go too far away to find a proper sea for yourself."

"They're all proper. They all fit."

"Fit?" Mrs. Larkin asked. Hannah shrugged and did not reply.

Mrs. Larkin smiled warmly and reached across her desk and patted Hannah's hand. "You're just starting, my dear. The sky is the limit here. Or perhaps I should say the sea's the limit." Mrs. Larkin laughed gaily, but Hannah smiled quietly to herself and touched the pouch beneath the bodice of her dress.

Now Hannah looked up at the Clock Tower. The hands were at twenty-five minutes before nine. Hannah had made a detour on her way to the interview on Beacon Hill to come by the harbor. She was not due at number 18 Louisburg Square until nine o'clock, but she would get there five minutes early. That would impress them. Promptness was essential in domestic service.

Mrs. Larkin had given her a handbook to read about how domestic servants — from scullery girls to butlers — were expected to behave. Hannah had almost memorized the book, reading and re-reading the sections on why girls were dismissed. The reasons were fairly clear — all of which, from drunkenness to stealing, were listed under the heading of "Inappropriate Behavior." Most of it was clear and easily avoided, but there was one short paragraph that disturbed her. Mrs. Claremont, the author of the book, had written, "Of course, if a servant appears eccentric or odd, or for one reason or another just does not seem to fit in the household, she can be let go. Usually if this is the case, a severance payment is made."

Money or no money, *severance* was a harsh word. Hannah knew what it meant. Dismissed, discharged, cut off. She simply could not be cut off. For cut off now might mean being sent away, far, far from Boston. Far from the salt air of the sea.

NUMBER 18
LOUISBURG SQUARE

HANNAH MADE HER WAY up the steep brick sidewalk of Mount Vernon Street, which bordered the west side of Louisburg Square near the top of Beacon Hill. Four rows of stately redbrick houses around the square looked down on a gated, leafy park. Mrs. Larkin had told her that number 18 would be on the far side of the park, the third house from the right. She stopped and counted in three houses to find number 18, which was almost identical to all of the others. There was a disturbing rigidity to the overall design — the flat fronts, the lines of shutters painted a dark green that appeared almost black. Hannah could not help but think of the ominous words of Mrs. Claremont in the book: "Of course, if a servant appears eccentric or odd, or for one reason or another just does not seem to fit in the household, she can be let go. Usually if this is the case, a severance payment is made." *I* will *fit in!* Hannah thought, and marched resolutely up the walk to the front door of number 18.

Hannah was happy that number 18 was one of the few houses with a bowed front. It gave the house a more welcoming appearance. Like all of the houses, number 18 had a tiny front yard with a low wrought-iron fence. In the middle of the yard was a tree bare of leaves but with visible buds that appeared swollen in anticipation of spring, though it would be another week until the beginning of March.

In the middle of number 18's door there was a brightly polished brass lion's head clutching a large *H* in its mouth. Hannah lifted the *H* and tapped it against the plate of the door knocker, which also had an *H* inscribed on it. She waited the better part of a minute, but no one appeared. She knocked again, louder. Still there was no sign of movement. Hannah tipped her head toward the heavy, carved door and pressed her ear against the wood, straining to hear through it.

Just then there was a loud creak and the door swung open. She tumbled against something firm.

"Ooh! Ooooh! I'm so sorry."

"I should think so . . . what in the name of — ?"

Oh, no! How could I have forgotten. Back door! The thought coursed through Hannah's head too late. Had she not read in the handbook Mrs. Larkin gave her that service people must always use the service entrance at the back of the house? Within the first ten seconds, before she had even entered the house, she had succeeded in making herself an ill fit. A dozen words flew through her head. *Abnormal, weird, outlandish. Yes, there's a good one*, she thought. *Might as well just hang a signboard from me.* OUTLANDISH GIRL APPLYING FOR A JOB IN LOUISBURG SQUARE.

A very tall man was now brushing off his double-breasted frock coat. The small brass buttons were as polished as the door knocker, and the letter *H* gleamed from them.

"Mr. Hawley, I am so sorry!"

"I am *not* Mr. Hawley. I am the butler and you I presume are the girl sent from the home."

"Yes, yes, Hannah Albury." She started to hold out her hand but realized this was not a good idea and quickly stuffed it back in her pocket. "I meant to go around to the back."

"You meant to? Then why have you come to the front?"

"I . . . I . . . guess I got confused."

"You confused the front of the house with the back? My, my! Well, I suggest that you try again." With that he took her by the shoulders, spun her around, and marched her back through the front gate.

"Turn left at the corner. Take another left into the service alley. Open the small gate with the number Eighteen to the refuse yard and knock on the door. Florrie will admit you and we'll start all over."

Hannah did as she was told. She stepped into the narrow refuse yard. There were only number 18s painted on the bins and barrels. No *H*s. The door had no knocker, so she rapped loudly. She heard footsteps, and the door swung open. "Heard all about you already. I'm Florrie. Brilliant!" The girl had black hair that foamed around her head. Her cheeks were ruddy. "Follow me. Mr. Marston just about had a fit."

"It was so stupid of me. I don't know how I forgot. And I studied the book so hard."

"What book?" Florrie tossed the question over her shoulder.

"*Mrs. Claremont's Guide for Domestic Service.*"

"You can read?"

"Yes, they taught me at The Home for Little Wanderers."

"Oh," Florrie said curtly. Hannah bit her lip lightly. Another mistake! Another thing to mark her as odd. Many servant-class girls did not know how to read. They had had to leave school early. Now this girl, Florrie, would most likely think Hannah was putting on airs. Hannah would have to make a special effort to be very nice to her. But maybe she could repair the damage a bit. "I don't read very well. And I'm absolutely terrible with figures. Can barely add two plus two."

"Oh, I can," Florrie said, then added, "but Mr. Marston does all the adding and subtracting around here." She paused. "Including the firing, which I guess counts as a kind of subtracting."

Florrie laughed at her own joke, and although Hannah felt a terrible dread, she tried to laugh extra hard.

"You're very clever, Florrie." Then she made a kind of humorous grimace. "Hope I won't be subtracted."

Florrie turned to smile quickly. It was a friendly smile and gave Hannah a bit of hope.

They had been winding through a maze of back halls, many of which had open shelves with bins and canisters. It appeared to be an extended pantry of some kind. There were cooking smells, and soon they went through double doors and arrived in the kitchen.

"New girl, Mrs. Bletchley," Florrie announced.

"Be right with you, dear." A plump lady whose face was beaded with perspiration was leaning over a large pot and tasting something. "It ain't got 'nuff pepper." She sniffed. A small boy was scrubbing potatoes.

"Your scrubbing days might be numbered, Chauncey, and you can get back to your beasts," Florrie said.

"Not a minute too soon. There's tackle to be polished with the Hawleys coming."

"This way." Florrie nodded and held a door open to a small hall off the kitchen. Hannah followed her. Florrie then walked up to another door and tapped on it. "Mr. Marston, the girl's here."

"Come in."

The butler sat behind a desk, bent over some papers. Spectacles were perched on his beakish nose. He did not look up. "I'll leave you two," Florrie said and closed the door behind her.

"Take a seat, Miss . . . Miss . . ."

"Albury . . ."

"Ah, yes, here it is. Hannah Albury. Take a seat, Hannah."

Hannah knew from the way he said her first name that it was not necessarily a sign of friendliness but merely a designation. Like Florrie, she did not qualify for the formal address of "Miss" or "Mrs." Lower maids were always called simply by their Christian names. He, on the other hand, must be addressed at all times as Mr. Marston.

Hannah sat down. "Thank you, Mr. Marston." This caused him to look up. He pressed his lips together into a firm line. It was not a smile but Hannah tried to interpret it as a slight sign of approval. His pale blue eyes looked at her steadily. Then he leaned back in his chair and cleared his throat.

"Yes, well, The Boston Home for Little Wanderers says you are a responsible young girl. Quick to learn — except for an alarming failure to discern the front of the house from the back —"

"I am so sorry, sir . . . Mr. Marston. I knew better. I mean, I read that in Mrs. Claremont's book and I don't know how I could have forgotten."

"You've read *Mrs. Claremont's Guide for Domestic Service*?" His somewhat bushy, reddish eyebrows crawled up his forehead.

"Oh, yes, sir. Every page, sir. I read the part about lemon juice and baking soda for polishing, and starch mixed with borax for —"

Just then Mrs. Bletchley entered. "Mr. Marston, can you add two bottles of the sweet sherry to the wines and spirits order? I had completely forgotten the spring luncheon Mrs. H always gives and I have to get those fruits macerating."

"Ah, mustn't forget Mrs. H's spring luncheon. And then of course the symphony tea."

"Yes, that I remembered."

"This is Hannah, Mrs. Bletchley."

"Ahh, the new girl." She glanced at her quickly. "Poor Dotty."

"Yes, poor Dotty indeed," Mr. Marston echoed.

Hannah had no idea who poor Dotty was. She supposed there was a strong possibility that Dotty had been the previous scullery girl. Perhaps she had been pitched, but given the lugubrious tones in which they both spoke and their downcast eyes, she imagined something worse.

"She reads," Mr. Marston added.

"Well, she won't be needing that." Mrs. Bletchley now ran her eyes over Hannah. "You strong enough to lift a twenty-pound block of ice?"

"Yes, ma'am, I think so."

"Let me see your hands." Hannah held out her hands and Mrs. Bletchley picked them up, turning them over in her own plump hands, which bore traces of flour. "Well, they ain't seen much work. But your nails are neat and clean. Mind you keep them that way despite scrubbing the fire grates. We don't tolerate dirty nails around here even if you're hardly to be seen upstairs." She paused. "No boyfriends, right? We don't tolerate that sort of thing, either. We've gone through that before."

Mr. Marston tipped his head up a bit and sniffed as if a bad odor had suddenly seeped into the room.

Hannah was almost stiff with fear. She simply had to make this work, but was Mr. Marston sensing something in her? Hannah touched her chest and felt the pouch.

"No boyfriends," Mr. Marston said.

The idea seemed absurd to Hannah. She hardly had friends. Most of the girls her age had left by the time she had returned from Kansas. She would commit herself to spinsterhood on the spot if that was what it took to get this job. It wasn't the money, even though it would be nice to make enough someday to have a tiny cottage by the sea. But it felt as though her very life depended on getting this job. If she failed, where would she go, or worse, be sent? The word *severance* hung in the air in an almost tangible way. Like an ax it could fall and suddenly slice away any hope of living by the sea. Once again, Hannah touched her chest and thought of the tiny glistening fragments in the pouch. She pressed her lips together and tried to calm herself as she looked first toward Mrs. Bletchley and then back to Mr. Marston. *Please, please*, she prayed. *Let me just seem normal. Let me fit.*

"I think it'll fit."

Hannah almost jumped when she heard the word. *Fit! I fit!*

"She be about the same size as Dotty, so her uniform might fit you." Mrs. Bletchley stepped back now and surveyed Hannah from head to toe.

"I was thinking the same thing myself, Mrs. Bletchley," Mr. Marston said. Did this mean she was hired? Hannah was about to ask, when Mr. Marston stood up and pulled a string that was behind his desk to unfurl a window shade on which an elaborate chart was drawn. Emblazoned at the top of the chart in bold letters were the words HOUSEHOLD STAFF NO. 18 LOUISBURG SQUARE. The chart showed a multi-tiered scaffolding, headed by the word BUTLER and followed by two other titles: COOK and HOUSEKEEPER. Then beneath them were half a dozen other positions, ranging from governess to valet to ladies' maid. All of these upper-tier titles were written in bold letters. There were at least a dozen or so others written in smaller print below, including the handyman, chambermaids, parlor maids, and kitchen girls. Hannah wondered where her place might be in this intricate construction.

Am I hired? That is all I really and truly want to know, Hannah thought desperately.

Mr. Marston began to speak. "What you must know is that this house in which we live is divided into two universes — that of the upstairs and the downstairs. The upstairs is the world of the Hawleys, the biological family that lives here. The downstairs is the work family. That is us, the serving staff. As the Hawleys are related through blood, we are related through work. Just as Mr. Horace Hawley is the head of that family, I, Samuel Marston, am the head of the work family."

Mr. Marston reached for a pointer propped against the wall and underscored his name with the tip. "My duties," Mr. Marston continued, "pertain to hiring and dismissing staff, managing the household budget, et cetera. But I need not inform you of all the details. There are rules that apply to both families. My job is to tell you the ones that are the concern of the downstairs work family. The number one rule is that downstairs family members are only to be upstairs for their work. One does not go upstairs for any reason except at the time of retirement. All female staff members who serve as maids live on the premises and use the back stairs to ascend to their sleeping quarters. While working we do not engage in conversations with the upstairs family unless specifically asked a question. There is no such thing as idle or casual conversation between the work family and the Hawleys." Mr. Marston stepped back and gazed at the chart as one might admire a beautiful painting. "This is our structure, the order, the hierarchy. Mrs. Bletchley has full command of the kitchen. Miss Horton, the housekeeper, sets the cleaning schedule."

It was a great deal to take in. Hannah's head was swimming with the details of the elaborate chart, the multiplicity of rules that seemed to govern every action. It was dizzying, but she could restrain herself no longer.

"Mr. Marston, I do not mean to interrupt. I hope that I am not violating a rule." Mr. Marston cocked his head and looked at her attentively. "But does this mean that you are hiring me?"

"Yes, it does. It does indeed. But before you agree to join our family, to become a citizen of our little nation, you must understand the laws that govern our citizenry. You shall be here" — he tapped the very bottom of the chart where there were two words — *scullery girl*. Above that position were at least a dozen others. "There are ranks and privileges associated with all these servants. For example, Susie, who is just above you, will supervise your vegetable scrubbing — is that not correct, Mrs. Bletchley?"

"Yes, sir."

Mr. Marston stood up. "It will be hard work. But you will learn to take joy and pride in your work no matter how low your rank is." He gestured at the elaborate chart. "There is nothing quite so satisfying as a job well done. That is what service is all about. We will send Willy with a cart for your things."

"I have no things, sir. Just a satchel. I can get it myself."

"Good. Be back in two hours. The Hawleys arrive tomorrow. Their ship docked in New York two days ago and they'll be on the Thursday train. The five-oh-five. There is much to be done in the next . . ." Mr. Marston reached in his waistcoat pocket, drew out a watch on a chain, and popped open the face cover. "Yes, as I was saying: there is much to be done in the next thirty-one hours and thirty-five minutes!"

TWO VASES

THERE WERE MANY THINGS that Hannah did not understand during her first days at number 18 Louisburg Square. Not the least of these things occurred late in the afternoon of her arrival.

"Quick! Quick! They're coming. We must be in the front hall," Florrie said, rushing into the scullery pantry off the kitchen.

Hannah was confused. Were the Hawleys arriving early? "Fetch the vinegar and the lamb's wool cloths. Third shelf and to the left. I'll get a bucket of water. Meet me in the front hall."

Who's coming? Hannah wondered. *And why in the name of heaven do we need vinegar and polishing cloths to greet them?* Certainly Florrie and she weren't expected to polish the Hawleys or any guests who might be arriving.

"Who is it, Florrie?" Hannah asked five minutes later as she came into the front hall with cloths flung over her shoulder.

"The vases," Florrie said.

The front door stood wide open despite the light drizzle outside, and Hannah saw that Mr. Marston was standing at attention on the front steps as a dray pulled by two sorry-looking horses drew up along the curb. Florrie was right behind Mr. Marston, but a step inside the house to avoid the rain. "Mr. Marston, I can never remember how you call them vases, that Japanese name."

"The Kirayhasi vases, by the potter of the same name from Kyoto, Japan."

"They're coming all the way from Japan?" Hannah said.

"No, just Paris," Florrie replied. "The Hawleys always travel with them wherever they go. Ain't it so, Mr. Marston?"

"Yes, indeed. This is the vases' sixteenth Atlantic

crossing." Mr. Marston now turned around to the half dozen servants who gathered in the front hall. "All right, we want a clear path for the men. Miss Horton, are you prepared to man the corners and are Willy and Johnson here with their tools? Stepladders in place? Cleaning fluids at the ready, Florrie?"

"Yes, sir!"

Miss Horton stepped toward Hannah. She had a long, thin face with a pinched look about her nose as if she were always seeking the alien scent of uncleanliness. There was a scoured look about her, and Hannah imagined that she regularly subjected her body to scrubbings with the most abrasive cleaning agents, and then rewarded herself with a bath in a solution of bleach and borax powders. She was as skinny as a stripped birch limb and nearly as white. Her hair was skinned up and twisted into a tight knob on top of her head. The cords of her neck were pronounced and rose from the stiff black collar of her dress like a bundle of twigs.

When Miss Horton began to speak, her mouth reminded Hannah of a drawstring purse. "There is a particular way that we clean the vases upon their arrival. I shall explain and you can watch Florrie. We begin generally with a thorough dusting using the feather dusters. Stepladders don't bother you, do they, dear? You're steady? Because if you're not, please tell me. We'll get someone else for the task. This is very important. Nothing — I repeat, nothing — must ever endanger the vases. They are this family's pride and most important possessions."

"No, ma'am. I'll be fine."

"Good then. Let us all stand back and watch the arrival."

A hush fell upon all the servants as eight men came up the steps bearing two long crates, four men to each crate. Through the slats Hannah could see a tapering object wrapped in burlap.

Mr. Marston had taken a post just inside the entry hall and was walking backward, his arms held high in the air. "Steady there, watch the left side. That corner takes a sharp turn, down the hall past the morning room on the right, and into the drawing room on the left."

"It's so exciting," Florrie whispered. "The vases! It means the family is really coming back." Hannah looked at the faces of the other servants. Their eyes gleamed, and despite the grayness of the day, a nearly ecstatic light bathed all their faces. She supposed this had something to do with Mr. Marston's idea of service. She remembered how his voice had been almost tremulous when he had spoken of the satisfaction of a job well done. "That is what service is all about," he had said.

Mrs. Bletchley sighed softly. "Well, now everything's back to normal."

Hannah couldn't help but wonder if she would ever feel this way. Could she ever share in the pride that seemed to envelop every single servant as this peculiar ritual was completed, a ritual that seemed so central to this household? *They live for this household,* she thought. *It is their only life.* But could it be her only life? She had once walked by a store near The Boston Home for Little Wanderers that had a ship in a bottle on display. It shocked her. How could one stuff a ship, an ocean, and the wind that drove that ship into a bottle? The ship had looked stifled, gasping for air.

"Now, come with me, girls," Miss Horton said. "While they are uncrating the vases, I'll explain to Hannah about their care." Hannah and Florrie followed Miss Horton into the drawing room. Both crates were lying on the hardwood floors while Johnson, the handyman and carpenter for number 18, pried up the nails with Willy, his assistant. It took them no time to have the vases out of the crates and the debris removed. Then Mr. Marston withdrew a long pair of scissors. The servants stood back as he flourished them and walked around the wrapped vases that lay like two shrouded corpses on the gleaming wood floors. He circled them once, then twice. "I am considering beginning at the base for my initial incision. Then I propose a medial cut at a forty-five-degree angle." As carefully as a surgeon in an operating theater contemplating the removal of a major organ, he gazed at his patients.

Miss Horton was now crouching at one end. "Would it help if I loosened these top swatches here?"

"Yes, yes, good idea. And knife, please, Mrs. Bletchley." He paused. "You did bring the gutting knife?" Mrs. Bletchley sniffed and stepped forward.

"Yes, sir."

"Please stand by until I call for it."

Florrie leaned over and whispered to Hannah, "Mrs. B hates her knives being used for anything but kitchen work. Says it ruins them."

The endless yards of burlap and canvas bandages were cut away. The operation took nearly twice as long as moving the crates into the house. Now Hannah could see the lovely blue designs against the white porcelain — a bird in flight, a tree, some low shrubs, and clouds.

"This is the scary part," Florrie whispered as Mr. Marston took out several pairs of rubberized gloves from his apron. He handed a pair to Willy, another pair to Johnson, and then put on a third pair himself. "That's so their hands won't slip when they raise up the vases," Florrie said softly. "This is the only thing that Mr. Marston ever lifts that's heavier than a magnum of champagne." Hannah had no idea what a magnum of champagne was.

What ensued was like a silent dance in which each dancer knew his part to perfection. At a nod from Mr.

Marston, the three men stepped forward. Johnson held the base steady. Willy slipped his hands under the midsection and Mr. Marston supported the slender neck with both hands. On a nearly silent count of three, the vase rose and was then transported the scant few feet to its position on one side of the wall facing the fireplace. The second vase soon followed to the other side of the wall.

Mr. Marston stood back. "Good work, all of you. Miss Horton?"

"Yes, sir." The housekeeper stepped forward with a tray that had a decanter and three small glasses. Mr. Marston poured some amber liquid into each glass, then handed one to Willy and one to Johnson, and took one himself. He turned around to face the other servants. "To a job well done. Safe again at number Eighteen."

"Hear! Hear!" someone said.

"What are they drinking?" Hannah asked.

"Sherry. It's the only time they ever drink upstairs. Mr. Hawley gave them permission. Each time the vases come home, they have a toast. Just the men, though — the ones who lift them up. But the dray drivers get a handsome tip from Mr. Marston."

"Very nice, Hannah," Miss Horton said, examining the patch of porcelain Hannah had just dusted. "Now come down and we'll move the stepladder around toward the back of the vase and you can begin there."

The vases were more than eight feet tall, and Hannah had to maneuver her stepladder around and climb it carefully. That was when she saw the design of the tail breaking through the curling waves. Her heart skipped. "What's this?" she whispered to the vase. Her breath fogged a small patch of the crashing wave. Only a tail was visible from the cresting water. The rest of the fish was obscured by a froth of foaming water. But was it a fish? This tail seemed to suggest something infinitely feminine and lovely. The flukes had gracefully sweeping contours that evoked beauty and power — an incredible power. Then something else caught her eye. The scales of this creature had a familiar shape, flat, not quite oval. Her breath locked in her throat. She closed her eyes and felt the weight of the pouch on its string beneath her dress. *It couldn't be!*

"Hannah, are you finished dusting? I'll pass up a bowl of vinegar water and a sponge."

"Just a minute, Miss Horton." Hannah moved her duster slowly over the tail, wondering if the vase Florrie was working on was identical.

Miss Horton handed up the bowl of water. "Squeeze the sponge out completely, because if there's too much water, there will be streaks. Can't have that," the housekeeper admonished.

Fifteen minutes later the job of washing the vases was complete. While Florrie took the cleaning fluids and sponges and dusters back to the pantry, Hannah excused herself to go to the servants' privy. She was desperate to look at the crystals contained in the pouch, in particular the one that had been transformed into an oval shape. In the dim light of the privy, she loosened the drawstrings of the pouch and shook the contents into the palm of her hand. "A teardrop," Hannah whispered. "Just like the ones painted on the vase." She closed her eyes again and tried to think. One thing she knew for sure. She could not let this mystery distract her from her work, her job. It was crucial that she do her work well, fit in, and never give them reason to question her dedication to the smooth running of number 18.

Supper was served in the servants' dining room, off the kitchen. Except for the fish chowder it was a cold supper, as Mrs. Bletchley had been too busy preparing for the Hawleys' return to do anything "fancy," as she called it, for the servants.

Mr. Marston stood at the head of the table. Mrs. Bletchley was to his right, and he did not begin to serve until she had seated herself.

"The dollhouse arrived, too?" Mrs. Bletchley asked as she sat down.

"Yes. All in good order."

"The dollhouse?" Hannah turned to Florrie.

"Ah," Mr. Marston said. "You didn't see the dollhouse yet, Hannah?"

"No, sir."

"The dollhouse is as important in its own way as the vases, and has made almost as many trips back and forth across the Atlantic. You see, Hannah, although the Hawleys spend a great deal of time abroad, they feel their true home is here in Boston. As the girls started coming along, they didn't want them to forget their house on Louisburg Square. So Mr. Hawley commissioned an exact replica of number Eighteen. Craftsmen were hired to copy all the furnishings, the oriental rugs, even the vases in miniature. It is a wonder to behold and the girls still play with it. Florrie and Daze are in charge of its cleaning and setting up. I suppose you'll be doing that tomorrow morning, won't you, girls?"

"We've already started cleaning it, Mr. Marston," Daze said.

"That's good. There is always so much to do, isn't there?" Mr. Marston replied as he dished out the food and passed the plates.

"Yes, so much." Mrs. Bletchley sighed. "Tomorrow night I promised a nice big cod. I'll send Willy down to T Wharf. Mr. Curtis already has my order."

"Mr. Marston," Hannah said, turning to the butler. "Might I ask a question about the vases?"

"Certainly. What question do you have?"

"Is there a story with the vases?"

"A story?" Mr. Marston said. "You mean a history? I believe they were made sometime in the last century."

"No, not that kind of a story. I mean the paintings on the vases — the birds, the waves, the fish tail — do they all tell a story?"

"Maybe it's a Bible story," Johnson offered. "Jonah and the whale."

"I don't think it's a whale story," Hannah said softly.

"What kind of fish tail do you think it is, dearie?" Mrs. Bletchley asked. "Not a cod. I'll tell you that. No cod or salmon has scales like that." They all laughed, except for Hannah, who touched the place on her chest where the pouch hung.

"You can't tell because the rest of the fish isn't really visible," Florrie offered.

"Perhaps it's a myth of some sort," Miss Horton suggested.

"Perhaps," Mr. Marston said and then slapped the table lightly. "Now, I suggest that we all turn in early." He once again pulled out his watch from a vest pocket. "For as I said, they shall be arriving on the five-oh-five tomorrow. That gives us twenty-one hours and thirteen minutes. And tomorrow morning the trunks will be arriving in advance on the first train. The girls' rooms are ready?"

"Oh, yes," Miss Horton said. "Lila's is thoroughly dusted. All the water closet items vinegared. We'll do another spraying of rose of attar on the bedsheets. She shan't have reason to complain. If I hear so much as a sniffle coming from her this time, I swear it will be the devil's work!"

"We need not swear, Miss Horton," Mr. Marston gently admonished. "This is a Christian home. I am sure you and Daze and Florrie have done admirably."

The conversation had quickly switched from the vases to the subject of Lila Hawley, the eldest and apparently most delicate of the three Hawley daughters. "But," continued Mr. Marston, "we don't want her looking all blotchy from hay fever as I believe Stannish Whitman Wheeler, the new young artist who is quite the talk on both sides of the Atlantic, has been engaged to paint the girls' portrait while they are here in Boston this spring." A chorus of *oohs* followed.

"Who is that?" Hannah asked.

"Stannish Whitman Wheeler" — Mr. Marston turned to Hannah — "at the tender age of nineteen has emerged as if from nowhere as one of America's foremost portrait painters. He has painted portraits of the finest families in America, England, and France. The Hawleys have engaged him to paint, as I understand it, a group portrait of their three lovely daughters — Lila, Clarice, and Henrietta. He started sketching them in Paris this winter. The painting is to be completed here."

An artist! Hannah thought. She had never met an artist. It was hard to believe that someone could make a profession out of painting pictures of people. He must see differently, feel differently. It was hard for Hannah to imagine someone like that entering the rigid and unbending world of number 18.

THE ROOM AT THE TOP

THE DRIZZLE HAD continued and a thick night fog had rolled in, casting an eerie, gauzy whiteness on the square so that the dark was not really darkness. Gaslights hung like luminous pearls over the sidewalk, their stands having dissolved into the mist.

Hannah stood, looking down from her narrow, gabled window, wondering what the three sisters would be like. Lila, she knew, was of a delicate constitution and Clarice was supposed to be the prettiest as well as the most serious. Henrietta, the youngest, seemed to be the favorite of the staff. The girls didn't go to school, but had a governess who traveled with them. And there had been quite a bit of talk about

Lila's debut the following year at Christmas, when she would turn seventeen.

Earlier that day Hannah had helped Florrie prepare the vinegar and lemon solution to wash down the bedroom. Several times she had heard Lila's hay fever mentioned, but there seemed to be more to her condition. The words *high-strung* had been often used. But then again the servants had talked of Mrs. Hawley as being high-strung as well. *Terrible expression*, Hannah thought. It made her think of bodies twitching on the gallows.

She turned now and looked at her room. It was the first time in her life she had not had to share, except when she was out in Kansas at Reverend Stubbs's house and had been too sick to appreciate it. But she wasn't sure if she appreciated this room, either. The milky light from Louisburg Square washed in, bleaching the dark wood pale and making the sparse furnishings appear almost insubstantial. *Ghostly*, she thought. *That's it!* She walked quickly out of the room and turned down the hall to the little alcove where a makeshift curtain had been strung.

"You asleep yet, Florrie?"

"No." Florrie pulled the curtain and sat up on her mattress in the cramped little space. "What is it?"

"She died in there, didn't she? Dotty died in my room," Hannah said.

Florrie blinked. "Not in it."

"What do you mean?"

"She was ill there. They took her to the charity ward of Mass General Hospital. She died there."

"But she haunts it."

"No . . . I mean I never seen her or nothing like that. It's just that . . . Oh . . ." She struggled for the words. "She ain't no ghost if that's what you mean, Hannah."

"Why do you cram yourself in here and give me the big space?"

"I just ain't comfortable there. She was a strange girl anyway. I never did like sharing the space with her and when she got real sick, I moved here. I like it better. That's all. Now, don't worry. Go to sleep. You have to get up earlier than any of us so you won't be spending much time there, anyhow." Florrie pulled the curtain, and Hannah could hear her nestling down into her quilts on the squashed-up mattress.

Hannah found small comfort in the fact that she would hardly be spending much time sleeping in the room. She might not sleep at all if some ghost of a dead scullery girl began gallivanting about. But there was little she could do about it. It was not thoughts of Dotty or ghosts that disturbed Hannah's sleep that night, but the lingering images painted on the two vases. Just as she was on the crest of sleep, Hannah would think of that breaking wave on the vase with the tail rising from the foam. She could almost hear the sea crashing and she felt something stir deep within her. Something familiar, yet so distant. Perhaps ghostly, in an odd way.

She wasn't aware of actually thinking *I must see that vase again.* She just rose from her bed. She felt a keenness, a sense of agitation and apprehension as she made her way silently down the four flights of stairs. When she entered the drawing room, the gas-lights had been turned down so that there was only a dim hovering glow, a tiny soft halo within each globe. But the milky fog outside seemed to wash into the room like a tide of pale light settling softly on the furniture. She felt a strange yearning rise in her. The stepladders were gone. She did not dare move anything to climb on so she might see the tail better. But was she too short?

She walked up to the vase she had dusted that afternoon. She could easily see portions of the body just before the tail began, and she could see the teardrop shape of the scales. Her heart was beating wildly as she drew the pouch from beneath her nightgown. She loosened the drawstrings again and this time shook out just a very few of the teardrop-shaped ovals. Taking one, she held it up to the scales painted on the vase. It fit perfectly, shimmering against the porcelain with a slight iridescence that pulsed once and suddenly seemed to magnify. The glimmer soon spread over the entire vase, enveloping it in a luminous glow.

Hannah pressed her cheek against the cool porcelain of the vase. She felt herself grow calm. She stood for perhaps two minutes with her cheek and her palms touching the curve of the vase.

When finally she looked up, the tail was closer than she thought. It brushed the crown of her head. She had wondered before if the creature really was a fish and if it was male or female, although there was something that suggested femininity. All that wondering seemed unnecessary now. It was not exactly a fish in any definable way. But it was female, of that she was sure, and it seemed very powerful. It had to be powerful, for the artist had depicted a storm-lashed sea yet this creature was swimming easily through the waves, not simply easily but almost joyously. She looked up at the way in which the tail flipped from the crest of the wave. Whatever the creature was, it looked free, utterly free!

She pressed her mouth close to the vase now and whispered as if speaking to some spirit contained within it. "What just happened? Is it me? Did I make this glow?" But there was only silence, and her whispered words spiraled into the soft vaporous radiance that had spread from the vase and begun to steal across the room. As soon as she tucked the crystal back into the pouch, the glow began to fade, like a tide ebbing back to sea.

Hannah stayed another few minutes then went back upstairs to her room on the third floor.

During the night, a land breeze came up and swept the fog back out to sea.

It was not a dream. That was Hannah's first thought upon waking. She knew that last night had really happened. The crystals in the pouch were not mere ovals, but perfect replicas of the scales of the mysterious tail on the vase. Hannah's head had begun to blur, and then it struck her with a great force. *I have broken a rule!* The number one rule Mr. Marston had laid down was that Hannah should only be in the family rooms for work.

Yesterday, Hannah had felt truly blessed that she had a place to live near the sea, and soon would have a dollar and three quarters in her pocket. But she had risked it all last night. Had she been caught, she would have been summarily dismissed without so much as a cent. The question was, how had she forgotten? Her recklessness chilled her blood. *Think! Think, Hannah! Think before you do anything so foolish again.*

THE PAINTER

THE NEXT MORNING, the house was a beehive of activity. As soon as Hannah had finished polishing the front-door knocker and took her rags and polishing paste back to the kitchen, Mrs. Bletchley called out.

"Change out of your scullery uniform and put on upstairs clothes. They needs you on the third floor to help with the trunks."

"I don't have an upstairs uniform," Hannah protested.

"Oh, yes, you do. We keep spares for the scullery girls. Go down past the silver pantry to the first door on the left. Dotty's is hanging there. It's got her name on it."

Hannah went to the closet. There were three hangers with Dotty's name. One had a black dress, one a pink, and one a lilac color. Each had a different apron. Which one was she supposed to wear? Hannah had no idea. She rushed back into the kitchen.

"Which one, Mrs. Bletchley? There are three."

"The lilac one, of course."

Hannah blinked. She wasn't sure what was so "of course" about it, but she hurried back and scrambled into the uniform. She was trying to fasten it when she heard footsteps. It was Mrs. Bletchley. "I'll help you with the fastenings."

A minute later Hannah had tied the full-length white pinafore apron around her and put on the upstairs regulation maid's hat, which looked like a pancake with a frill around it. Mrs. Bletchley measured her approvingly. "Well, the apron's not pressed, which wouldn't do if they was here, and you've got the cap on cockeyed." She straightened it out. "All right, now run upstairs and help Daze and Florrie with them trunks. Miss Horton will direct you."

On the third-floor landing, Hannah nearly collided with Florrie, who was obscured by a huge, fluffy cloud of crinolines. "Go to Lila's room, Daze is there."

"Which is Lila's room?"

"Last on the right, just after the nursery."

Hannah peeked into the nursery as she walked by. The dollhouse was set on a low table, an exact replica down to the lampposts on the sidewalk. She couldn't resist going in for a closer look. Hannah crouched down on her knees. It was empty of furnishings, but even so, she had never seen or imagined anything like it. Everything from the wallpaper to the gas lighting fixtures were identical to the real ones except in miniature. She even found her own room, tucked in at the very top of the house under the narrow dormer.

"Come along now!" Florrie stuck her head into the nursery. "I'll let you help me with it later. But Daze needs your help getting these clothes organized."

Hannah got up and followed Daze into Lila's bedroom. Never had she seen such a lovely bedroom. The bed was hung with a gossamer canopy embroidered with flowers that exactly matched the ones painted on the headboard. The curtains matched the canopy and there was a lovely thick carpet with gold-colored fringe. On the dresser were delicate porcelain figurines of animals. Across from the dresser, there was a writing desk with gilt edges and an array of elegant pens set in silver holders at the edge of a blotter. A white and gold plant stand that spilled with pansies and ivy stood by the desk. *Pansies already!* Hannah thought.

"Whatcha be gawking at, girl?" Daze said, looking up from the trunk she was already unpacking. She was plump with a rounded, dimpled face and a delicate spray of freckles that spanned her nose and cheeks, giving her a naturally rosy appearance.

Hannah had been trying to place Daze's accent ever since she had met her the previous day. It was very odd. Not really Irish. There were so many Irish children at The Home that Hannah had even been able to pinpoint if they spoke with the clipped cadences of County Clare or Sligo, County Kilkenny or Kildare. Daze's speech was clipped, but then it suddenly seemed to swoop up at the end of words or sentences only to be chopped off almost with a hiccup.

"I'm gawking at everything! I've never seen such a room. It's like a princess's." Hannah looked around. It was hard to imagine that all these beautiful things were for just one girl, only one year older than herself. She bet that the furniture and all the gewgaws in this one room cost more than the fabled one thousand dollars that Mr. Marston earned in a year.

But if Hannah had a little seaside cottage, she wouldn't need any of this. She would have shells for decoration and no curtains so she could watch the sea day and night. And she would not have nearly as many clothes. Indeed, although her terrible rash was gone, she remembered how free it had felt to wear no undergarments. She had never felt "depraved" as matron had suggested.

Daze snorted, "Yeah, that what Miss Lila be, a princess, if not a queen. See that heat stove over there in the corner?"

"Yes." There was a small porcelain coal-burning stove that was painted with delicate flowers.

"It's a copy of one that belonged to a famous French queen — Marie Antoinette, the one that went and got her head chopped off."

"Ooooh! Who'd want one like that?"

"Not me, but we ain't Miss Lila, are we? She's a little strange. And it be your job each evening when the family is having dinner to scurry up here and start a fire in it to warm the room, so it be nice and toasty when Miss Lila comes to bed."

"And what's that tiny little bed?" Hannah asked as she caught sight of an exact replica of the larger bed with the same canopy, even down to the miniaturized version of the embroidered flowers.

"That's Jade's bed."

"Who is Jade?" Hannah wondered aloud.

"A cat. And she's not that small for a cat. She's a big, fat thing. And that, my girl, is one of your first lessons."

"Yes?"

"No one except Miss Lila ever touches Jade. None of her sisters. Not Mr. or Mrs. Hawley. Not Miss Ardmore, the governess. No one. But it be your job to bring a pan of milk up for Jade when you come to light the fire. Now come here and help me."

Daze began with a rapid-fire list of instructions. "Take these to the laundress for immediate ironing. Miss Lila likes her chemises and combis arranged in stacks of four in the middle drawer. So when you bring them back, remember, stacks of four. Line up her shoes in her closet according to this chart." Daze handed Hannah a carefully drawn diagram that had a small drawing of each shoe and showed the order of where it was to go on the shoe rack in the large closet that was as big as Hannah's room. "And never, never ever touch the figurines. Only Miss Horton is allowed to dust them."

"Why's that?"

"I told you, she's strange . . . bit weird in the head." Daze looked up and tapped her maid's cap.

"I heard someone say she was high-strung."

"That be one way to put it, I s'pose." Daze turned her back and began sorting through petticoats.

"Are the others that way, too?"

"No. Pretty normal for girls so rich and spoiled.

Clarice is very sweet, but she takes holy hell from Lila just for being so pretty even though she's three years younger."

"And what about Henrietta?"

"Oh, Ettie?" Daze laughed. "Ettie's something else!"

"What do you mean by 'something else'?"

"Ettie's just nine. Bit of a tomboy. Look, dear, I ain't got no time to go explaining them to you now. You'll see they all be as different as can be. But you gotta be careful of Miss Lila."

As soon as Hannah had delivered the clothes to the laundress, she came back up to the nursery. Daze was on her knees, surrounded by boxes with labels on them. "Do you read?" she asked.

"Yes."

"Good, that will be helpful." She laid her hand on a stack of boxes to her left. "These are the people boxes." She began to unstack them. One label said UPSTAIRS MAIDS, HOUSEMAIDS, AND DOWNSTAIRS MAIDS. Another said COOK, MR. M, SCULLERY. Then there was a box with the word FAMILY on it. Another box was labeled FIRST-FLOOR CARPETS AND PAINTINGS. There were at least twenty boxes filled with the furniture, decorations, and people figures, all part of the household at 18 Louisburg Square. They put the plump doll with the gray curls and cap in the kitchen at the range. That was Mrs. Bletchley. Then they hung up all the pots and pans. Next they slid the miniature wine bottles into the racks in the wine cellar and stood Mr. Marston in front of them.

For Hannah, the dollhouse was an education. In the brief time she had been at number 18, there were many rooms she had not even seen. For three hours, Daze and Hannah dusted, polished, and sorted out all the contents of the dollhouse. They began hanging the pictures in the downstairs rooms and putting out the Oriental carpets that sparkled like tiny jewels. There was even a set of the vases, but the paintings on the vases were crude in comparison to the real ones downstairs. The crashing waves had a rigid geometry and the tails of the sea creatures seemed to droop, devoid of energy or power. It was as if the artist had tried to reduce the entire ocean and its creatures to a single drop of water.

"Oh, dear, here's poor Dotty." Daze sighed as she unpacked one of the servant boxes. "Well, I guess that's you now," she said, and put the small figure up in the room on the top floor. "You don't mind, do you?"

Hannah was caught aback. She looked at the servant figure dressed in the same rough-woven skirt that she had been wearing earlier, with an apron that even had smudges of coal dust. "I do sort of mind, Daze. Could we change her a bit?"

"Good idea! We have spare uniforms. We'll just put her in an afternoon upstairs one and, you know, I have a great idea." Daze jumped up and went to a cabinet with paper, paints, and brushes. "Dotty had blond hair. It will be easy to dye her hair with some of these India ink paints and make it red like yours."

The girls fussed with the doll for nearly a quarter of an hour. "Look at her!" Daze said, propping the doll against a miniature coal scuttle. "Pretty good job, eh?"

"Very good. Thanks," Hannah said and began to reach for another box.

"Don't touch that!" Daze blurted as Hannah started to lift the lid from the box that was labeled LILA'S BED-ROOM. Hannah's hand froze above the lid. "Nobody is allowed to touch or clean the furniture for Lila's room in the dollhouse. She even has a little china cat that looks just like Jade in it."

"All right," Hannah said. "What about the other girls' rooms?"

By two o'clock they had finished and Hannah had changed back into her scullery clothes and been sent to clean the grates and lay the fires in the first-floor rooms.

Now she walked into a room she had never been in before. As soon as she entered, she stood very still. Hannah recognized it as the music room. Daze had arranged its furniture in the dollhouse version. There was a grand piano and across from it, beside two very tall glass-paned doors that looked out on a garden, stood a harp. Hannah set down her scuttle of coals and kindling. The colored strings, the shapely contours, the very gleam of the harp's wood drew her. She had never seen a harp before except in pictures. There was not another soul in the room and the harp stood solitary in a shaft of morning light. Although there was no player, Hannah sensed a stirring in its strings. But how could this be? The harp was untouched, and yet Hannah could feel or almost hear a quivering of fragile sound, like a melody waiting to breathe.

Suddenly Hannah sensed another presence in the room. She wheeled about and found herself facing a tall young man with thick black hair and eyes the color of emeralds. She gasped.

"I didn't mean to startle you, I'm sorry."

"Mr. Hawley?" But he was much too young to be the master of the house.

"Hardly!" The man laughed. "I'm Stannish Wheeler."

"The portrait painter?" She almost whispered the words. She was suddenly very nervous and could not meet those emerald eyes. It was as if they emanated a current.

"Yes, the portrait painter." He cocked his head to one side and narrowed his eyes as if to study her. He took a step closer, a pulse twitched in his temple, and the color drained from his face. Hannah was alarmed. *What is he seeing?* He looked as if he might faint.

"Sir, are you . . . are you well?" She reached out her hand as if to steady him, but he immediately took a step back and she felt herself blush furiously. *Stupid! Stupid! How stupid of me.* He was a big, tall, healthy man. Why would she ever think he was going to faint?

He shook his head slightly and seemed to regain his composure. "Nothing is wrong, nothing at all. It's just that . . ."

His voice dwindled off, but he continued to stare at her as if he were searching for something. The scarlet tide of her blushing had receded, but her heart was pounding, and her mouth felt dry. *Please, leave*, she prayed silently. *Just leave!*

She picked up her feather duster and began to sweep around the fireplace, although it was quite clean. "The family is not here yet. Not expected until later this afternoon."

"Yes, I know. I came to look at this room as a possible place to pose the girls."

She kept her back squarely to him and continued to sweep the nonexistent dust. "I think I heard Mr. Marston say that the portrait was to be painted in the drawing room in front of the vases."

"Ah, yes, I know. The precious vases!" There was something in his tone that suggested perhaps a faint contempt for the two vases. Hannah could feel his eyes studying her. "And you — what do you think of the vases?"

Something froze in Hannah. Slowly she turned about. "You don't think they're pretty?" Hannah asked.

"Oh, yes, the vases are very pretty," he replied. "But I wonder about trying to contain something as wild as the sea on the surface of a vase made of clay."

Before Hannah could stop herself, she replied, "Yes, it's like trying to cram a full-rigged ship into a bottle. I saw one once in a store window."

The painter tipped his head again and regarded her with renewed curiosity. "Precisely. Some things can't be contained."

But that of course was precisely what Stannish Wheeler did, thought Hannah. He was a portrait painter. He put life on canvas, or at least tried to.

"Nonetheless," he continued, an odd, tight smile playing across his face. "I'll wager that you think the vases are beautiful and are most especially drawn to that tail breaking through the crest of the wave."

Hannah felt her blood run cold. He reached out to touch her arm, but she turned away. "I am sorry if I have offended you in some way. Please, forgive me."

Hannah fought against touching the pouch beneath her dress. It had become somewhat of a nervous habit. But the painter must not see her do this — if he saw one touch, he would know too much about her. Already it was as if he had intuited that she had crept down the stairs to where those vases stood sentry, two mystical guards of some unknown world.

In *Mrs. Claremont's Guide for Domestic Service* one of the most important admonishments was to never enter into conversation with guests of the house, except if needed to serve. Hannah pressed her mouth shut. Mr. Wheeler did not need to know what she thought of the vases. Any explanation of her thoughts was outside the job requirements.

"Ah, Mr. Wheeler!" Mr. Marston said, entering the room. "Well, you have had a look. But I seriously doubt the Hawleys will agree to a change of venue. You know, the vases and all."

The painter pulled his gaze away from Hannah. "Yes, I understand, Marston, but tell me one thing. If indeed the Hawleys have carried the vases back and forth across the Atlantic numerous times —"

"Sixteen times to be precise," Mr. Marston cut in.

"Yes, and also take them to their summer home in Maine, why would they not move them from one room to another?"

"That is really not for me to say, Mr. Wheeler." The silence was broken only by Hannah arranging the kindling in the fireplace.

"Yes, I understand," Mr. Wheeler said. And then she heard them both turn and walk from the room.

I am like glass to him, like water, Hannah thought to herself, alone now in the music room, heart racing. *He sees through me, but how?*

THE RIVER

STANNISH WHITMAN WHEELER'S composure disintegrated as soon as he reached the bottom of Beacon Hill. He stopped and leaned against a lamppost, closing his eyes. "It simply cannot be. It cannot be!" he murmured, then shook his head as if to banish the wild thoughts that were swirling in his brain. As he stepped out to cross Charles Street, he was nearly run over by a hansom.

"Watch where you're going, idiot!" the driver yelled as he swerved the horse to avoid him. "Wanna get yourself killed?"

"Maybe!" Wheeler muttered.

He continued across Charles Street and entered a neighborhood known as lower Beacon Hill, where the hill flattened into a small nest of streets bordering the Charles River. He turned onto Brimmer Street, and walked a short block to the building on the corner where he lived and worked in an apartment on the top floor. The rent was reasonable and the light was good, for it faced north. But most important, he could see the river.

It was the same wherever he went, be it Boston, London, Paris, or Florence. The only thing that changed was the name of the river — the Charles in Boston, the Thames in London, the Seine in Paris, the Arno in Florence. Always a river. A river that flowed to the sea.

But now it was as if the sea had flowed back to him. He sank into his armchair in front of the window and took his customary posture. His elbow propped on one arm of the chair, his chin resting in his hand. He watched the river, observing the play of light on the water. Sometimes the water seemed like a gray satin ribbon unspooling toward the sea. Sometimes, like this day, the first bright, sunny one after long drizzling weeks, it flowed like a liquid rainbow. He liked it in all its moods, although he sometimes detected a tint of mockery in its shifting reflections.

He had been stunned when he entered that music room and she had turned around. How could he have expected such a thing? It was not that she was beautiful. But he had known the moment he entered the room, before she had even turned around, that there was something . . . a fluid grace in the way she bent toward that coal scuttle. *Does she know yet? Or maybe it is the other way around, maybe she has chosen . . . no . . . no . . .* , he argued.

Stannish now entered a complicated internal argument with himself. She had made that remarkable observation about the vases — how had she put it — like trying to cram a ship in a bottle? That remark alone would suggest that she had not made the choice; that she was ignorant, or rather, innocent.

It was all too complicated. He could not refuse the commission. He had already started the portrait. The Hawleys were one of the most important families here in Boston and prominent in Paris as well. Not only that, but the portrait was to be displayed at the Paris

Salon, the most important art exhibition on either side of the Atlantic. Hervé, his dealer in Paris, would kill him if he backed out. But how could he continue in the household? Perhaps he would not see her that much. She was definitely not high on the staff, a parlor maid at best.

Finally the voices in his head ceased. He gazed out at the river and made his decision. "I am a great painter. I am on the brink of getting everything I've worked for. And I know all I have given up."

BLOOD AND MILK

"**Them tarts, you put** a berry right in the center of each and mind you really get it in the center, Susie. Hannah can help you."

The Hawleys had arrived promptly on the 5:05, and now at almost eight they were just sitting down for dinner. Hannah had never heard of anyone eating supper, which they called dinner, so late. In the three hours since they had arrived, she had not caught a glimpse of a single Hawley. This apparently was her destiny, not belonging to that exalted order of upstairs maids, like Florrie and Daze, or Miss Horton, the head housekeeper, or Roseanne, who was Mrs. Hawley's personal maid.

As soon as Hannah had finished helping with the dessert tarts, Mrs. Bletchley reminded her that she should go kindle the stove in Lila's room and take the pan of milk "for that creature." Hannah carefully ascended the back stairs balancing the milk pan in one hand and the kindling scuttle in the other, wondering why Mrs. Bletchley called Jade "that creature." The stairwell was quite dark with only very dim gaslights on the landings. Just before she approached the third-floor landing, she caught a glimpse of something pale and milky white flowing silently through the darkness. Her heart skipped a beat. *Dotty! No. No ghosts.* She had slept in Dotty's bed undisturbed. Hannah swallowed and took a deep breath. "Stupid you are! Stupid, stupid, stupid," she scolded herself in a muttered whisper, and walked forcefully and somewhat loudly up the last half flight of stairs to the landing.

"Ah!" said a voice when she reached the landing. A large woman stood at the head of the stairs. She was not just large, but voluminous. Her skirts billowed from her ample hips, and her bosom jutted out like a promontory. But she had a friendly face, with cheeks that swelled into bright red crab apples and a perfect tiny bow mouth. She was uniformed but not aproned, a significance not lost on Hannah. Miss Horton did not wear an apron either. The lack of an apron indicated that a servant was of the highest ranks in the upstairs world. *This must be Roseanne*, Hannah thought, though she hardly fit the part of a lady's maid. With her ruddy face, she looked more suited to scaling fish down at T Wharf. But Florrie had told Hannah that Roseanne was one of the most coveted ladies' maids in Boston and the only staff, aside from the governess, to travel to Europe with the Hawleys. Efficient and skilled with a needle, she could mend anything, repair lacework, and she possessed an immense archive of recipes for removing any kind of stain.

"Coming up with her nibs's dinner, I take it," she called down.

"Yes, Jade's milk."

"You should use the dumbwaiter, dear. Less chance of spilling."

"It was occupied. Mrs. Bletchley was sending up dessert from the kitchen to the dining room."

"Oh, just ask her. People bend over backwards to keep Jade happy, not to mention her mistress,

Miss Lila. I'd like to wring that damn cat's neck and turn Lila over my knee and give her a good hard spanking!"

"Oh!" Hannah inhaled sharply and nearly spilled the milk.

"Well, get along with you, dear, and mind you don't cross the cat. Her claws are something fierce. She's got six toes, you know."

Roseanne turned and went down the hall the opposite direction from Hannah. Gusts swirled in the wake of her large body and its wide skirts. A rose in a slender bud vase trembled and dropped a petal as if in homage to its human namesake.

All the gaslights were lit as Hannah made her way down the hallway to Lila's room. The door was half open. As she walked in, she heard a low tearing sound, like fabric ripping. She spun around, milk sloshing over the edge of the pan. Facing her was the most enormous white cat she had ever seen. It stood in front of the porcelain stove, blocking her way. Arching its back, it made the ripping noise again. Hannah froze as the cat fixed her in its slitted stare.

She now realized why it was called Jade. Its eyes were like twin gemstones.

Hannah instinctively knew that this was not the kind of cat to be called with a "Here, kitty, kitty." She bent down and slowly set the pan of milk on the floor. The cat did not deign to look at the pan, staying firmly rooted to its spot with its back arched and its hard gaze locked on Hannah. A piercing blue-green light emanated from its eyes and seemed to focus with burning intensity on the spot beneath Hannah's uniform where the pouch was concealed.

The cat hissed and arched its back higher. Hannah felt it might leap across the room and tear at her throat. The cat was blocking the door to the stove grate, but Hannah took a step closer. The cat blinked. A gold vertical slit flashed through the jade gleam.

One minute passed, then another, without the cat moving a fraction of an inch.

"She was expecting Dotty." The voice came from behind. There was a flow of white as Jade stirred and Hannah knew it had not been a ghost on the stairs, but Jade.

Hannah turned around. "Begging your pardon, miss, she would not let me get to your stove."

Standing in the doorway was a slender girl a year older than Hannah, the cat now in her arms. Lila Hawley buried her chin and nose in her pet's thick fur and settled her eyes on Hannah. Hannah gave a little gasp. Four hard gemstone eyes locked her in their gaze.

"You're the new scullery girl, aren't you?" Lila Hawley spoke through the fur.

"Yes, miss, I am."

"Do we like her, Jade? She came to light our fire. We should let her do that, shouldn't we, Jade?" She spoke in a low voice that seemed to gurgle up from the back of her throat. The sound was not unlike the ripping noise the cat had made, but softer, quieter. "We'll let her light the fire. Yes." She paused. Then she stuck out the tip of her tongue and licked Jade's nose. "Oh, and I know what you want. You smell it, don't you?"

Lila walked toward where Hannah had put down the pan of milk. She crouched down and looked at

Hannah while she kept talking. "Yes, Mummy's brought you a special treat and no one is going to know our little secret. Scullery girl won't tell." She drew a wad of newspaper out from the deep pocket of her dress. Jade was now out of her arms and crouching in front of the milk pan. Lila unfolded the paper and took two dark, gelatinous lumps into the palm of her hand. The cat was quivering in anticipation, and Lila's pale hand was dripping now with what looked like blood. She slipped the lumps into the pan and dark red swirls radiated through the milk. "We love our chicken livers, don't we. And nobody tells how we sneak them out of the kitchen when Mrs. Bletchley's not looking or that we bring them upstairs. And nobody's *going* to tell either, are they, darling Jade? Because Mama doesn't like me feeding you anything but milk upstairs. Dotty never told. And Hannah won't tell either. Will she?"

"How did you know my name, miss?"

"Oh, I always make it a point to learn all the servants' names, especially the scullery girls'." She had stood up now and walked closer to Hannah. Very close. Hannah took a step back. "Don't move!" Lila commanded. She raised her hands. The tips of her fingers were slimy with the blood. "Now turn around."

"Why, miss?"

Lila sighed deeply. "You're not supposed to question me. And besides, I'm doing it for your own good."

"My own good?"

Lila rolled her eyes in a show of exasperation. "You don't want me to wipe my fingers on your clean white apron, do you? I'll just do it on the hem of your skirt. It will never show. See how thoughtful I am?" The corners of her mouth pulled back into a tight little smile.

Oh, yes, and I'll have to wash out my hem every night, Hannah thought.

"As a matter of fact, just crouch down and start the fire up, and I'll wipe my hands while you lay the kindling and light the fire. That will be very efficient, won't it? Two tasks completed at one time."

Hannah shook her head in slight dismay but turned around, and began doing exactly as Lila had commanded. The faster she got away the better. While she was laying the kindling, she could feel the tugs on the hem of her skirt.

"Oh, Jade, guess who came for dinner tonight," Lila chatted. "Mr. Wheeler."

Hannah caught her breath. She had tried to not think about him ever since she had met him that morning in the music room, but now Lila was prattling on.

"He is the handsomest man in Boston. And he's going to paint our portraits. All of us together. I mean not Mama and Papa, but us girls. I wish it were just me. But Mama says if he does a good job on this, she'll have him paint one just of me. I mean the whole reason for us coming home from Paris is so Mama can plan my debut. And the whole reason for a debut is to introduce young ladies to society so that they might find a husband. So I think as soon as we decide on the debutante dress, Jade, that Mr. Wheeler should start painting me all by myself. I want an off-the-shoulder dress." The room seemed to resonate with this odd conversation and the soft noises of the cat slurping the bloody milk.

Lila dropped the hem of Hannah's dress and the fire started with the first struck match. Hannah couldn't wait to get out of the bedroom. She did not say good night. She merely gathered up the scuttle and her matches as quickly as possible. Lila was sitting on her bed, cuddling Jade and talking to the cat earnestly about her dress, her beautiful shoulders, and how boring Boston would be if it weren't for Mr. Wheeler and how she hoped he would come to Maine this summer when they went. Hannah stole a glance. A nimbus of gold light from the overhead fixture enveloped the girl and her cat. But together on the bed they did not seem illuminated, but rather the center of a dark violence.

As Hannah started down the back stairs on the second-floor landing, she met Daze coming up.

"You got the fire going in Lila's stove?"

"Yes, but Holy Mother in heaven, she is strange!"

"I warned you."

"That cat!"

"Oh, yes. She and that cat. Quite a pair they are!" Hannah felt a tremor pass through her. "Lila sneaked up the chicken livers, did she?"

Hannah nodded and then said, "Do you think Mr. Marston knows?"

"Probably."

"And he doesn't tell?"

Daze sighed deeply. "Look, dear, Mr. Marston above all wants to keep what he calls a 'well-regulated house.' When Lila goes off, it's like a rock being thrown into the middle of a still pond. Peace is shattered. Everything starts to fall apart. Mrs. Hawley ain't the steadiest herself. So she goes into what they call 'a decline.' Then Mr. Hawley begins fretting and his heart ain't so strong. It's just bad all the way round. Understand?"

"Uh . . . yes, I guess so."

Hannah didn't really understand at all. And what disturbed her the most was this odd relation that Lila had with the cat. The cat was like Lila's imp, her demon spirit that made her whole. And then Hannah had the most shocking thought of all: to feel whole was a wonderful thing, a luxury. Did she actually envy Lila in some way? Something had come together in Lila that Hannah almost coveted.

She wished she could steal down to the drawing room and put her cheek against the coolness of the vase. If she closed her eyes, she knew that in the hollowness of the vase she would hear those timeless rhythms of the sea.

BECOMING INVISIBLE

THE DAYS WERE BUSY ones for Hannah, as the Hawleys had been away in Paris for a long time and were anxious to see their old friends in Boston. There were many dinner parties and teas, and when the Hawleys were not entertaining, they were attending parties in other people's homes, or going to the symphony, or to events at their clubs and the various museums and societies that they belonged to. There was much work for the staff. The poor laundress was kept so busy that a helper had to be hired to deal with all the ironing, bleaching, and starching. Hannah struck a truce of sorts with Jade, who more or less ignored her when she came up with the pan of milk. Lila never spoke to her when they encountered each other. The family, except for little Ettie, tended to peer right through Hannah when she came into the morning room to tend the fire. Hannah realized that she was becoming just what Mrs. Claremont's book equated with success in terms of domestic service — invisible to her employers. "It is only the surly, clumsy, sloppy, and dishonest servant who attracts attention," Mrs. Claremont had written. "The perfect servant becomes invisible to the masters of the house."

The only threat to Hannah's invisibility was Henrietta. Clarice, the middle Hawley daughter, was both beautiful and dreamy and could often be found with her nose stuck in a book. But it was nine-year-old Ettie who actually spoke to Hannah when she chanced upon her in one of the downstairs rooms.

One morning, as Hannah was laying kindling for a fire in the music room, Ettie came in with a small bouquet of flowers.

"Hi, Hannah, Mama said to put these in water right away and then set them on the little table."

"Is there to be a party in here?"

"Sort of," Ettie replied earnestly. She was a child who thought carefully about every word she said. Her hair was a dark chestnut brown. Her solemn gray eyes were set off by thick lashes. She had a little dimple that flashed playfully even when she said the most serious things. And despite Mrs. Claremont's several admonishments against engaging in nonessential conversations, Hannah often found herself talking with Ettie.

"Now, what do you mean by 'sort of,' Ettie?"

"I think there's supposed to be some musical performance."

"Does anyone ever play the harp, Ettie?"

"Not really that much anymore. There used to be a lady in Maine who played it, but I think she died. We have an even nicer harp in Maine. But I think Aunt Alice is coming tonight and she sometimes plays the harp."

"I've never heard one," Hannah said.

"Never heard harp music?" Ettie opened her eyes in wide astonishment.

"No, never."

"It's lovely music, the music of angels they say. Although I think angels are sort of boring."

Hannah laughed. "Is it to be a big party tonight?"

"I'm not sure. And I am considered too young to go. But I know Mr. Wheeler's coming. So that means Lila is going to spend forever in the bathtub and Clarice shares that tub with her and will be really mad as it is her first grown-up party in Boston. But you know, Lila, she has a terrible crush on Mr. Wheeler, and oh, I nearly forgot! He starts painting us tomorrow and Mama said to be sure my pinafore dress is pressed. Lila wants to wear something that Mama says is much too daring for a girl her age." A mischievous gleam came into the gray eyes. "You know what I mean, Hannah, very naked-looking. I think she wants to look almost naked for Mr. Wheeler!" She giggled.

"Oh, hush now, Ettie. That's not a proper thing to say."

"Maybe I'm not a very proper girl," Ettie said. She smiled and the dimple flashed.

"I'm sure you're very proper, Ettie."

"No," she said, suddenly serious. "I'm just nine. I think you can't really judge if a person is proper or not until they get a little older." Her forehead now creased and she looked at Hannah intently. "I mean it's like when children do naughty things, that is just what it is — naughty, misbehaving. But you have to be older to be judged improper or proper. It's as if there is this whole set of rules for older people, grown-up people, that are, in a way, harder to understand and if you break them, it's not that you are simply bad, but you are not proper."

Hannah stood up from the fireplace and put her hands on her hips. "Ettie, for a little girl, proper or improper, you do a lot of thinking, very complicated thinking."

"I like thinking," Ettie replied gravely.

And I do, too, thought Hannah. Proper for Hannah in this world of the Hawleys meant complete invisibility, clean uniforms, knowing how to pare a radish to Mrs. Bletchley's specifications — tulip-shaped in spring, roses in summer, winter, and fall.

Suddenly Ettie's face brightened and all the solemnity fled from her clear gray eyes. "Hannah!"

"Yes?"

"I've had a minor brainstorm!" She tapped her temple lightly with her finger.

"About manners and what is proper?"

"Oh, no, no. Nothing so boring. It's my braids."

"Your braids?"

"Yes, my braids." She touched her two fat, glossy braids. "Miss Ardmore braids my hair every morning. She hates doing it and yanks so hard. She's always angry, or I should say seems angry in case you haven't noticed." Hannah had noticed that Miss Ardmore, if not outright angry, did seem slightly vexed all the time. But it was not really pronounced at all and Hannah was yet again surprised by young Ettie for detecting such subtleties of behavior. "It's as if these braids of mine were made as the perfect objects for her anger — I mean a vent for it. Hannah, I am going to ask Mother if you can braid my hair from now on! Brilliant, isn't it?"

Ettie did not wait for an answer. She just ran from the room with her brilliant idea.

When Hannah went downstairs, Mr. Marston was discussing with Mrs. Bletchley that evening's dinner menu. He then turned to Miss Horton and spoke about the china that was to be used. "And not the Georgian silver. Mrs. H feels it's too heavy and ornate for this time of year, and the same for tomorrow night's dinner party even though it will be slightly more formal — and — ah, Hannah, for tomorrow night Mrs. Hawley wants yellow tulips, French style. The florist on Pinckney has reserved masses of them. I can't spare Willy to help you get them. So tomorrow it will take you two trips, I fear. Too bad they didn't come in today with the roses that she ordered for this evening."

"I don't mind, Mr. Marston. I'll be quick. Will I be helping with the table setting?" There was an awkward silence. Had she said something wrong? Hannah wondered.

"Oh, no, no, my dear!" Mr. Marston chuckled softly. "You're not quite ready for that. Maybe someday when you've advanced, but setting the table is a very precise operation." From a deep inside pocket of his waistcoat he drew out a ruler. "We measure everything, don't we, Florrie?" he said, nodding toward her and Daze.

"Oh, yes, sir," Florrie replied. "Wineglass, two inches from water glass. Napkins one half inch from fork."

"Excellent, Florrie!" He smiled quickly. "I think everything is going quite well. I must commend you all. The transition of the Hawleys' return from Paris has gone quite smoothly and I think we are all settling in. It is a well-regulated household, as it should be and will continue to be even when we go to Maine."

"And when will that be, Mr. Marston?" Florrie asked.

"I have no precise dates yet. But I would imagine that a small contingent of us shall be going up in early June to prepare Gladrock, as usual."

Gladrock was the name of the Hawleys' summerhouse in Bar Harbor, Maine. Hannah had seen a picture. It was an immense, sprawling shingle house. The first thing she had noticed was that it was close to the sea. The next thing that caught her attention was that there were so many chimneys poking up she could not imagine how many fires she would be laying. But no matter; it was a small price to pay for living within sight of the sea.

Hannah was in the morning room, where Mr. and Mrs. Hawley often had a second cup of coffee after their breakfast to discuss the day's activities. She was in her upstairs uniform, for she had been asked to go and polish the wall sconces. She was at the far end of the room and perhaps they had not even noticed her when they came in. But she heard a sound halfway between a sigh and a sob.

"Horace, what will we do? She's been so good and now she insists on the cat."

"Well, I don't think it's that bad, Edwina, I mean it's better than her in that dress she wanted to wear. It's a compromise. Compromises can be good."

"But a cat in a Stannish Whitman Wheeler painting. I don't know, it just seems wrong."

"Does he mind?"

"I'm not sure. He didn't say no. I think he realizes that she's delicate."

"Who knows, he might let her pose with it and then paint it out in the end if he doesn't feel it's right," Mr. Hawley said. "Remember how he changed the color of Bettina Lattimore's dress and painted out the bowl of orchids, prize orchids from her own hothouse? He has a mind of his own. But I think he generally gives people what they want. He doesn't want her looking grouchy in the painting."

"Certainly not. But do you really think he'll be that flexible? He did want us to move the vases into the music room."

"I know, and I put my foot down on that idea. But I'm not in the painting. So I won't look grouchy, and I can be a grouch, as you well know, my dear! I want the girls posed in the drawing room. This painting has to look like Boston. Not a Paris salon. This is Boston. We are Bostonians, despite spending so much time abroad."

"Well, what will a cat in the painting make us look like?"

"The cat is technically a Bostonian."

With this Edwina Hawley burst into fits of laughter.

"Oh, Horace, darling, you are a dear, funny man." It was at this point that Hannah made her escape through a rear door. If they had noticed she was in the room, they said nothing or didn't care. She had become invisible. She had two conflicting emotions. On the one hand it was a great boon not to be noticed. But she was like a piece of their furniture. There but inanimate, unfeeling. *I am nothing!* she thought. *Absolutely nothing! Was I not made for something more?* Hannah felt almost as bereft as she had on the train heading for Salina, Kansas.

When Hannah came back into the kitchen to change her apron for the downstairs chores, she saw Mrs. Bletchley going over a list with Mr. Marston pertaining to the evening's entertainment. Mrs. Bletchley was seldom without a list — either a grocery list, or a menu, or a list of tasks that must be completed for a meal preparation, or a schedule. She squinted at the paper and then slid her arm back and forth as if she were playing a trombone. "Susie, where are my specs?" A large part of Susie's job was keeping track of Mrs. Bletchley's specs, which she refused to wear on a chain around her neck for she felt it interfered when she was cooking.

"Here they are, Mrs. Bletchley."

"You're a dear, Susie," Mrs. Bletchley said, putting on the spectacles but still squinting at the list.

"All righty, now, Hannah, tonight you'll have to serve dinner in the nursery for Miss Ardmore and Ettie. I'm trying to have something nice for them because you know how Ettie gets her little nose so out of joint when she misses a big people's party."

"Oh, forgive me for interrupting, Mrs. Bletchley," Mr. Marston said. "But I forgot to tell Hannah that there is a slight change in duties. Mrs. Hawley has requested that you come up each morning after you have finished your downstairs duties to braid Ettie's hair. I believe it was Ettie's request, actually." From the corner of her eye Hannah saw Mr. Marston raise an eyebrow and give a slight nod toward Mrs. Bletchley, which seemed to suggest a hint of amusement mixed with approval. He then added, "What Miss Ettie wants she usually gets."

But Hannah wondered, would Mr. Marston approve if he knew that Ettie wanted to have "little chats" while she braided her hair? Would such chats be considered unnecessary conversation and confuse the borders that governed the worlds of the upstairs and the downstairs?

PROPER BOSTON

THE DAY SEEMED ENDLESS to Hannah. It was just six thirty in the evening and she was far from finished as she walked up the back stairs. She had just put the "nursery dinner," as it was called, on the dumbwaiter. As she opened the dumbwaiter door on the third floor, she could hear voices coming from the various rooms.

"Daze," Mrs. Hawley was saying. "Tell Lila that she has to get out of that tub now or there won't be time for Clarice to bathe."

Florrie rounded the corner, nearly obscured behind a pile of turquoise silk ruffles. "What's that?" Hannah asked.

"Miss Lila's dress. A Charles Worth original. Her first."

"Who's Charles Worth?"

"Just the most famous house of fashion in Paris," Florrie said.

Daze now came dashing back from where she had tried to pry Lila from the tub. "This is proving impossible. That girl!" she muttered.

Then Clarice came stomping out of her bedroom in her dressing gown and headed for her mother's dressing room. "Mother!" she said in a tone that was seldom heard from Clarice, who was normally quite complacent. "She says that she'll get out of the tub if you let her wear the emeralds."

"That's simply ridiculous. Emeralds are too old for a girl her age. She'll look like an old lady."

"I'll take care of this, madam," Roseanne said as she charged out of the dressing room. She emanated an air of authority that tolerated no nonsense, especially when it concerned her mistress, to whom she was very devoted. Hannah and Daze stood watching her in awe as she sailed down the hallway. With her wide hips swaying and her skirts swishing, she could have been a square-rigger running downwind with a robust breeze on her stern. Within one minute, Lila was out of the tub and Clarice was in it.

Roseanne came back down the hall, passing Hannah, who had come back with the second tray for the nursery. She gave Hannah a hot glance. "Emeralds, my arse!" Then she turned into Mrs. Hawley's room and in the refined voice of a ladies' maid said, "All in order now, Mrs. Hawley. Never you mind. She'll look lovely in that Worth gown, and Clarice's in the tub."

"Ettie! What are you doing?" Hannah whispered as she glimpsed the little girl peeking around the corner.

Her gray eyes sparkled. "Did you hear Roseanne?"

"Yes," Hannah answered.

"I just love it when Roseanne gets after Lila."

Hannah went into the nursery with the second tray of the nursery dinner.

Although the room had long since ceased to be a real nursery, it still had a few remnants from its previous life. There was, of course, the dollhouse, along with several of Ettie's stuffed animals, which she played with more than the dollhouse. A rocking horse and a shelf full of painting and drawing materials sat in one corner. "I think Mrs. Bletchley has a special treat for your dessert," Hannah said as she arranged the food on the table.

"Oh, how kind of her," Miss Ardmore said. "She always tries to make something special for you, doesn't she, when there is a grown-up party?"

"What would be special," Ettie said, "is if Mummy would let me come to the party."

"When you're older, dear," Miss Ardmore replied.

"Hannah must be my spy," said Ettie.

"Spy? Whatever are you talking about, Ettie?" Hannah asked.

"Spy . . . spying! I want to know if Lila makes eyes at Mr. Wheeler."

"Ettie!" Miss Ardmore exclaimed. "That's very vulgar."

"Vulgar for me to say or Lila to do?"

Hannah nearly dropped the tray. *This child!*

Miss Ardmore sputtered, "Ettie, I don't want you talking like that."

"Fine," Ettie said, and slid her eyes toward Hannah with a look that showed clearly what she expected from Hannah.

"Ettie," Hannah said. "You know I don't even serve in the dining room. I'm just in the kitchen. I won't see anything. And Miss Ardmore is right. Spying isn't nice."

Miss Ardmore nodded primly at Hannah as if to thank her. Of course she wouldn't actually thank her. Miss Ardmore rarely spoke to those servants who were not official upstairs maids. She clung fiercely to her unique status in this household; as a governess, she did not belong to the serving class. She indeed was quite thankful when Mrs. Hawley had relieved her of the onerous task of braiding Ettie's hair. She viewed it as a promotion of sorts but at the same time was slightly offended that she was being replaced by a scullery maid. She had offered to supervise Hannah for the first few mornings but Mrs. Hawley thought that was entirely unnecessary.

Miss Ardmore did not wield the power of a butler like Mr. Marston, nor did she possess the intimate knowledge of her mistress that Roseanne guarded like a miser. Though her wages were not as high as Miss Horton's or Mr. Marston's, she set herself above them. When she placed the advertisement in the *Boston Herald* offering her services, she wrote, "Competent to teach reading, writing. Proficient in French, piano, singing, and drawing. Able to assist the lady in domestic affairs on occasion. Willing to do anything not menial." For Miss Ardmore, worse than any plague or consignment to eternal damnation was her dread of being asked to perform menial tasks. She, like so many governesses, was plain to the point of drabness, and often lonely. She had no prospects — either romantic or economic — beyond winning a position in a respectable upper-class household.

"Well," Ettie said, ignoring Miss Ardmore but continuing her conversation with Hannah. "Lila can make eyes all she wants with Mr. Wheeler. But Clarice is much prettier."

Miss Ardmore stood up. "Henrietta Hawley, I insist that . . ."

Ettie turned to her and said, "I was just going to say that Clarice is so pretty, but still too young. She's just thirteen and he might be nineteen or even twenty. But she is so pretty."

"What about yourself, Ettie?" Hannah asked as she set down a plate of sliced bread and butter. "When you grow up? You're just as pretty." Miss Ardmore gave her a sharp look. Hannah knew that she had crossed a boundary. This was definitely a non-essential conversation. Miss Ardmore must have read Miss Claremont's book as well.

"Oh, no. I'm going to have the Hawley nose," Ettie replied.

"Now, whatever is that?" Hannah asked.

"Really, Ettie," Miss Ardmore broke in. "This conversation must stop."

Hannah quickly gathered up the tray to leave. As she walked out the nursery door, Ettie shouted after her, "It's that honking big thing Papa has smack between his eyes and his mouth!"

⚜ ⚜ ⚜

As Hannah came back upstairs to get Jade's pan of milk from the dumbwaiter, she saw Lila and Clarice about to make their descent. They both looked lovely. Clarice was dressed in a pink gown with seed pearls embroidered in a floral design. Her blond hair was done up with tiny silk roses tucked in the coronet of braids. Beside her stood Lila in tiers of turquoise ruffles. A diagonal garland of ivory satin bows spilled down the skirt from waist to hem.

Hannah gasped with amazement when she saw Lila. She looked much older than sixteen, and stood there proudly enjoying the effect she was having on Hannah. "You look . . . you look wonderful, Miss Lila," Hannah said. But at just that moment Mrs. Hawley came out of her room, looking not simply wonderful but magnificent in her Charles Worth white silk gown overlaid with a black, delicately scrolled embroidery that gave the illusion of wrought iron with its curving tendrils and vines. The off-the-shoulder sleeves and deeply cut neckline provided the perfect frame for the blaze of diamonds against her creamy skin. Her dark blond hair was artfully piled into a cloudlike confection with a few tendrils falling to graze her ears, from which sparkling diamond pendants hung. By comparison, her daughters looked as drab as governesses.

"Oh, Mummy." Ettie sighed. "You look so beautiful."

"Thank you, dear. And don't your big sisters look lovely?" Hannah waited tensely.

"Oh, yes! And, Lila, you look very grown up." Ettie paused and turned to Clarice. "And, Clarice, you look the same age, but prettier."

"Prettier than me?" Lila said, tipping her head and looking at her little sister. Hannah noticed that her tone was not harsh but almost pleading.

"Don't be silly. I mean prettier than Clarice usually looks with her nose in a book."

There was a titter of nervous laughter.

❧ ❧ ❧

"Quick, Hannah! We've got an emergency. Susie's taken ill." Mr. Marston rushed up to her. "You're going to have to help serve tonight. Into a formal uniform now! Quickly, girl. Daze will help you."

Hannah rushed to the pantry closet where the uniforms were kept. Daze was already standing by the closet door holding out a black alpaca-wool dress with long sleeves and high white stock collar for her.

"I'll look like a reverend in this," Hannah muttered. "My goodness, the collar is scratchy." It was odd but ever since Kansas, Hannah had been much more aware of which materials chafed and which were soft. Her bedsheets were infinitely softer than her muslin nightgown, so she had taken to sleeping in nothing. And she loved the feeling — it was so free.

"Don't complain," Daze said. "Do well at this and then when we go to Maine you might get to serve again, and you'll earn yourself a nice Christmas bonus if they keep you for fancy parties. Here, I'll help you into the apron."

"Ouch! That's way too tight. I can hardly breathe!" But the apron was not the only thing constricting her lungs. The realization that she would see the painter again hit her full force at the very moment Daze tied the sashes.

As Hannah started to pull away, Daze called out, "Wait, Hannah, your cap." She helped Hannah put it on. "All your hair's to be tucked under. Mrs. Hawley is insistent about that."

"I wish we didn't have to wear these. It makes it so hot!" And was she already blushing? What if she spilled something on him? Her hands were shaking and she wasn't even carrying anything yet.

"Well, we do have to wear them," Daze said, pushing an escaping curl back under Hannah's cap. "Now you're set," Daze said, taking a step back and giving her an appraising look. The mobcap was a confection of frills and had three streamers that fell down her back.

"I hardly feel set, Daze. I don't know the slightest thing about serving in the dining room."

"Don't worry, Mr. Marston and I will look after you. Stick close to me and just do what I do. A few rules, though. Always serve from the left, but fill water glasses from the right."

Hannah swallowed nervously and repeated in a whisper, "Serve left, water right."

She was shaking like a leaf when she entered the dining room, and could not even look up to see where Wheeler was sitting. She just had to get across a distance of about ten feet with the first course, a velvety oyster soup. *God, do not let me spill this*, she prayed. In all, there were sixteen guests. She would only have to deliver three bowls. Daze and Florrie would take care of the rest.

"Don't worry," Daze whispered. "It's all downhill after the soup. That's the hardest."

Thankfully Wheeler was not one of the three guests Hannah was charged to serve. Perhaps it didn't matter. She felt his eyes following her as she moved about with the soup course and then cleared the bowls on Mr. Marston's signal.

Between the soup and the following course, Hannah stood at her post against the wall next to Daze. Mr. Marston surveyed the dining table like a great bird stalking a marshland. No glass must go more than two-thirds empty. Rolls must be passed at just the right time. Plates cleared when the slowest eater had begun his or her final bites. It was a complicated sequence of events that demanded precision timing. How Mr. Marston kept everyone's needs in mind and so quietly told all the servants what to do was nothing short of miraculous. But what did it really matter in the long run? Hannah wondered. What would happen if there was a slipup in the complicated code of serving a dinner?

Hannah looked at the people around the table. They were among the wealthiest and most distinguished people of Boston, in the house of an old and distinguished family. She had heard Mr. Marston once call the Hawleys "Boston Brahmins," and when she asked what that meant, he said, "Noble." Yet their lives were constrained by a set of rigid dictates as repressive in their own way as all the rules she had lived under at the orphanage.

Lila and Clarice were the youngest in the room. For the most part, the other guests were vastly older than even the Hawley parents. All except for Mr. Wheeler, who was seated next to a desiccated, gray-haired lady with crepey skin gathered under her chin in drooping folds like pleated satin. Two of the women wore lofty ostrich feathers that plumed airily above their hairdos, but none of the women were as magnificent as Mrs. Hawley. The men were all in formal attire except for one very elderly man, whose clothes were so shabby and threadbare, and his bow tie so crooked, that his garb could hardly be considered "formal" and perhaps barely even "attire."

Clarice sat to her mother's left and Lila to her right. Mrs. Hawley watched them both carefully through the entire first course, monitoring their conversations.

"Professor Curzon," Clarice said, turning her sweet, delicate face toward the wrinkled, slightly unkempt gentleman to her left, "did you read the article in the *Daily Advertiser*?" Hannah noticed Mrs. Hawley wince at the word *article*. Daze had told Hannah that Mrs. Hawley worried about Clarice with her bookish ways appearing "too smart" for her own good, distracting from her natural beauty. But Mrs. Hawley absolutely blanched when Clarice continued, "The article was about Theodore Roosevelt and his —" She broke off suddenly with a bit of a jolt. Hannah guessed her mother must have kicked Clarice under the table. "Mama —"

"We don't need to discuss politics at the table, dear."

"It's about conservation, Mama. He wants to set aside land for nature preserves."

"Nature preserves! What a silly idea." Mrs. Hawley laughed gaily.

"But, Mama, I plan to join the Sierra Club."

"How lovely!" Edwina Hawley's mouth pulled into a glaringly bright smile, and she deftly changed the subject. "Speaking of parks, have you seen the tulips this spring in the Public Gardens? They are simply spectacular, and they say that the quince tree is blooming for the first time in ten years."

Clarice appeared slightly miffed but retreated into her usual shell of benign silence. She never sulked. Conversation resumed along the lines that Edwina Hawley obviously found more pleasant and appropriate. There were swift segues to the opera, the symphony, boating on the Charles, and Mrs. Jack

Gardner's "palace" that was under construction on the Fenway.

Throughout these conversations, Lila was definitely "making eyes" at Mr. Wheeler. Coy looks darted from her like small birds released from captivity. She asked him in a taut voice what dress he felt she should wear for the painting, which was to begin the next day.

"Do you think this dress would become me for the painting, Mr. Wheeler?"

"Well, it becomes you anytime, Lila," he answered diplomatically.

"Oh, is Mr. Wheeler to paint your portrait, dear?" the elderly lady with the crepey skin asked.

"Yes." Lila turned away and answered the woman. Hannah and Mr. Wheeler both stole glances at each other, and their eyes locked. The glance had lasted only a second, two seconds at the very most. Hannah did not blush. It was not a moment of embarrassment or discomfort. Quite the opposite, it was a moment of astonishing intimacy and familiarity, as if they had retreated to a separate room, a place far from where they actually were.

"And myself as well as Ettie, he is to paint us in the portrait," Clarice offered.

Mr. Wheeler quickly broke away from Hannah. "Yes, and we must consult with them. It's important to have a balance of color in such a portrait."

"Why?" Lila asked. It was a single word but there was something in the way she said it that brimmed with defiance. The desiccated lady blinked and her pale gray eyes seemed to bulge out slightly. Professor Curzon became extremely involved with cutting his meat. Another woman appeared fascinated by the etched leaves on the water glasses.

"Lila." Mrs. Hawley turned toward her eldest daughter. There was a quaver in her voice. "Mr. Wheeler is one of the distinguished painters of today."

Lila dipped her chin slightly and then very slowly pivoted her head in her mother's direction. With a voice as steady as her mother's was tremulous, she said softly, "Then as the foremost painter in America he should know why."

Conversation simply stopped. A young girl at a formal dinner party had thrown down a gauntlet of sorts, challenging not simply the painter but all the unspoken rules of civility. Her tone toward her mother was unmistakable — cool but seething with contempt.

Hannah and Daze exchanged nervous glances. A desperate light seemed to flicker in Mrs. Hawley's eyes.

Mr. Wheeler coughed slightly. "Lila, as a painter it is my job to create a palette that tells the truth about the subjects of the paintings, that reflects the deeper currents running through their natures. At the same time, I must create a balance in the tonalities despite your and your sisters' individual characteristics."

Lila sighed, and then began to speak in a flirtatious, almost chirpy voice. "Well, I hope with all this talk of balance and tonalities, it will be flattering."

"I don't flatter. I only tell the truth," Mr. Wheeler said quietly. He slid his eyes toward Hannah.

MUSIC!

"Is this the new fashion, eh? Something from Paris, Edwina?" the elderly, rumpled gentleman asked.

Edwina Hawley smiled. "I have never liked this custom of the men going off to smoke cigars and the women withdrawing to a different location. This is 1899, the last year of the nineteenth century. Believe me, in the next century this habit will be gone. Out the window!" She laughed gaily. "Now into the music room. We shall serve coffee there, and after-dinner cordials with a bit of music."

When all the guests had been served, Edwina Hawley stood up. "And now I have begged Auntie Alice to play us a tune on the harp." She looked toward the old lady with the crepey skin.

Every morning since Hannah had been at number 18, she had come into the music room to stand in front of the harp and wonder what sounds could be drawn from it. Even in its silence, she could almost catch the elusive, fluid notes. Now finally she was about to hear it. A quietness settled upon her as the elderly woman took her place on the stool and tipped the lovely instrument back so it rested on her shoulder. The first chords shimmered in the candlelit glow of the room.

Water! This is the music of water. Not sky, not heaven, not angels, but water. The sounds of the harp spilled like liquid into the room. But it was not simply water, there was color as well. Hannah watched the woman's long fingers coaxing music from the strings. She knew the woman was good, but could she not draw out an even more delicate sound? If she would only let the string vibrate a second longer. Unconsciously Hannah started moving her own fingers over the edges of her apron. The liquid shadows of this music filled her.

There were only two people whose eyes were not on the harpist. Stannish Whitman Wheeler saw again what he had suspected when he first glimpsed Hannah in this room. He could not tear his eyes away from her, as if she had a resonance more powerful than any harp. He remembered the way the light had caught her hair that first morning he had come across her in this very room. *Could she be?* he asked himself for perhaps the twentieth time. It was impossible. But . . .

"What's wrong with Lila?" Daze whispered to Florrie. "Look at her staring at Mr. Wheeler." Florrie turned her head and inhaled sharply. Lila Hawley's face had been transformed into a peculiar mask as she watched Stannish Whitman Wheeler's rapturous gaze fall upon Hannah.

"MY OWN HEAVEN"

"**What would Mr. Wheeler** call the truth?" Lila Hawley buried her nose in Jade's fur as she stood before the oval mirror in her bedroom and admired herself. She was wearing just her underclothes and she slipped off the straps of her camisole to bare her shoulders.

"What is the truth about these shoulders, Mr. Wheeler?" she asked the mirror, angling first one way and then the other. There was only the flickering light of a candle. She made coy little gestures, winking at her reflection, casting sly looks over her shoulder, puckering up her lips into a little rosebud for an imaginary kiss. "Shoulders like these don't need to be flattered by your brush, do they? They're perfect.

Why, the no-count count, as Mama called that man who came to call in Paris, compared my complexion to a Greek goddess's. But now come to think of it, where has he ever met one? They're just made up. And why would I want anything to do with that old count? He had hair growing out of his ears! Why would I, Jade?"

She drew the cat close to her face. The cat and the girl peered into the mirror. Lila could see her reflection in the polished gemstone eyes of her cat, and Jade could see her reflection in her mistress's eyes.

"No, of course we don't want him. We want you know who!" She giggled softly and the cat purred. "He talks about truth, but what is truth? Is truth that stupid new scullery girl? I don't know." Lila sighed. "She does make me nervous. Now, with Dotty, you could trust her. Very docile. Remember the time when Mrs. Partridge lost her diamond clip and we found it? Well, Dotty, I guess, really found it but we kept it and I made her swear never to tell. And she didn't. Dotty was a good secret keeper. And now we have the clip. Oh, I'm going to get it from its hidey-hole. Let's play dress up, Jade!"

Lila put the cat down and walked over to the chimney where the porcelain stove's pipe connected. Lila crouched and slipped in her fingers to find a loose brick. Jade walked about the room as if patrolling it, defending the mistress's territories.

"Ah! Still here!" Lila drew out a small tissue-paper bundle. Jade walked over and began nosing the paper. "Patience, dear, patience!" After a few seconds Lila lifted from the nest of tissue a dazzling diamond clip that spiraled like a swirl of stars.

"Here, dear, you can wear it first." She took a thick tuft of the fur that grew between Jade's ears and snapped on the clip. "Oh, my! Don't you look absolutely beautiful!"

She scooped up the cat and walked over to the mirror and held her up. The candlelight was caught by the innumerable facets of the diamonds that cast reflections all about the room until the walls and ceiling danced with swirling galaxies of light. Lila began to turn slowly.

"My own heaven. I have made my own heaven right here. I am the goddess of it all" — she paused — "and my shoulders are flawless!" She stopped suddenly, cocked her head, and looked at the mirror. "You know what? I bet that stupid girl's shoulders have freckles. She's a redhead. Redheads always have freckles. Someday I'll find out. What would Mr. Wheeler think of that — a girl with ugly freckles all over her?" She began to giggle and her giggles erupted into shrill, high-pitched laughter. It ricocheted in her brain so loudly she thought her head might split and she put down the cat to clamp her hands over her mouth so no one would hear. She was laughing so hard tears squeezed out from her slitted eyes. Jade purred deeply and rubbed up against her leg.

"KNOW YOUR PLACE, SCULLERY GIRL"

HANNAH HAD TRIED her best not to think about Mr. Wheeler. And then there he was at dinner that evening, and made that stunning remark, "I don't flatter. I only tell the truth." He had been answering Lila but looking directly at Hannah.

It was as if Wheeler knew a truth about her she did not. The feeling grew in her during the after-dinner entertainment in the music room. She did not have to look at him to feel the peculiar sensation of his attention focused on her. It was as if that current she had experienced the first time she had met him tugged on her like those liquid shadows of the music.

That night Hannah dreamed of the harp's music. In her sleep, she touched the strings she had longed for. Her fingertips played a dream harp as real as the one three floors below. She knew instinctively how to persuade the strings to yield the notes, how to let the vibrations travel so that music, spinning like gold, wove through the air. Her body ached with this music. It wrapped around her like shimmering liquid shadows in her sleep. She felt the timeless rhythms of water, of tides, of the currents that stirred in the depths of the ocean. And when she was in the deepest part of sleep, beyond the reaches of the conscious world, where one's spirit can rise in the night air, she felt a rumble stream through her being. She woke up.

Outside a spring storm raged. The small window of her room rattled and she knew immediately that it must be a nor'easter. Usually these storms came in the winter with heavy wet snow but this was a spring one. Thunder shook the roof, but amidst the cracks of lightning and the rumbling of thunder, there was another sound. A vibration separate yet seemingly responding to the cacophony of the storm, a resonance that rose through the house like a single silver thread. No, not a thread — a string!

Hannah had a clear mental image, as if the reverberating object were right before her in the darkness of her room. It was the harp. She threw back the covers, swung her bare feet to the floor, and left her room.

For the second time she had violated one of the most important rules of the house, but she barely gave it a thought as she entered the music room. There was a loud crack and a filigree of lightning was framed in the panes of glass behind the harp. Hannah could see the strings quivering. The very air around the harp seemed to flutter as if stoked by hundreds of invisible midnight butterflies. As if in a trance, Hannah walked toward the harp. *I can make music*, she thought. *I can!*

She sat down on the stool. Very gently she eased the harp back so it rested on top of her right shoulder. As Hannah closed her eyes, the memory of the woman's fingers on the strings came to her. She curled her hand so the fingers rested lightly against her palm and her thumb lay on top of them. The strings of the harp grazed her knuckles. Then very slowly she opened her hand and placed her fingers, except for the smallest, on four strings and lightly plucked them. The harp's subtle vibrations became something else — a pattern, a wave of motion with depth and texture. Swirls of sound floated through the air.

She had played for less than a full minute when suddenly she was aware of a presence. There was a tiny sharp click that pricked the sounds swirling through the room and shattered the brief harmonies. She felt a tingle go up her spine. A crack of lightning illuminated the room, and the grotesque shadow of a cat sprang across the hot flash of white, followed by a strident ringing as Jade leapt onto the piano, unleashing a wild crash of notes. Hannah froze. The cat bared her fangs and screeched.

Jumping from the stool, Hannah raced from the room. She was not sure if the cat was following or not. She took the stairs two at a time. The skies opened up and a raucous roll of thunder obliterated the sound of her footsteps. She finally reached her room and slammed the door.

Sinking against the door, Hannah could hear nothing but the pounding of her own heart wild with fear. She shut her eyes tightly. How could she have been so reckless? But how wonderful it was — just those few seconds when the notes had been released into the air. It was as if she had crossed over into another world — a liquid, floating world where she fit. She latched the door and was determined to banish the horrid cat from her thoughts. She would go to bed and remember those few notes and her fingers — yes, the wonderful feeling of her fingertips on the strings. Hannah was amazed by that brief moment, and yet it had felt very natural, as if this music, those few notes were a gift that had always been within her but of which she had never been aware.

By the time the storm pushed out to sea, Hannah was sound asleep, and even when she woke the next morning she still felt wrapped in the harp's music. The rest of the Hawley household was in a less than harmonious state.

"Miss Lila be having one of her fits," Daze reported as she came in from the breakfast room with a tray.

"She says that she won't come downstairs when Mr. Wheeler comes to paint the portrait. Ran back upstairs right after breakfast."

"Oh, for heaven's sake. What is it this time?" Mrs. Bletchley huffed over a pot of oatmeal.

"The cat?" Susie asked.

"Yes, the cat." Miss Horton entered the kitchen. "Seems that Mr. Wheeler does not like the idea of painting Jade any better than Mr. and Mrs. Hawley do. He says it will throw off what he calls 'the chromatic balance of the painting.'" She sighed. "Whatever that means."

"I think, Miss Horton," said Mr. Marston as he came into the kitchen. "The word 'chromatic' is most often used in terms of music, the notes that belong to a scale of the key in which it is written." Mr. Marston enjoyed indulging in lengthy, professorial disquisitions on subjects. It gave him particular pleasure to do this in front of Miss Horton, who of all the servants in the household was closest to him in terms of rank or status. "But Stannish Whitman Wheeler is remarkable for the subtle, nuanced layering of color in his painting. The girls, have they not all been dressed in rather dark shades of mauve, gray, and violet? The vases themselves loom tall and alabaster white with their fine filigree of blue figure painting. Now throw a big, fat, snowy white cat into that palette . . . well, it is going to spoil all that. Unbalance things."

Miss Horton gave him a look of undisguised contempt. "That's a lovely theory, Mr. Marston. But you and I know we've got trouble brewing."

Mr. Marston at once looked chastised. His face turned grim. "You're right, Miss Horton. Forgive my digression."

Hannah spoke up now. She felt a bit sorry for Mr. Marston, and his theory sounded very learned to her. "I remember, sir, last night in the dining room Miss Lila asking Mr. Wheeler about the dress she was wearing and him saying that she should talk with her sisters about what they were wearing because it was appropriate to have a balance of color in the painting."

A slight frown creased Mr. Marston's brow. "Yes, very astute of you to understand this essential balance, but, Hannah, it is not appropriate that you listen in quite so carefully to the dinner table conversation and repeat it with commentary."

Hannah's face swam with confusion. "I don't understand, sir. I was only doing the same thing you were when you talked about the big, fat cat spoiling the chroma . . ." Her voice dwindled away.

"Not quite the same, Hannah, but you will learn. Now, don't worry too much. It's a rather chilly morning. So make sure the fires in the drawing room are lit well before Mr. Wheeler arrives."

"Yes, sir," Hannah muttered. *Some thanks I get for trying to defend him against Miss Horton.* The stupid rules of Mr. Marston! If he had only known what she had been up to last night in the music salon before that loathsome cat had appeared. Suddenly the entire household seemed so silly to her. It dawned on her in this moment that what she had loved so much when she heard the harp's music and then began to play in the midst of the storm was this sense or suggestion of a place, a world without such rules. A place where boundaries simply did not exist, but living things moved freely, in a limitless space, and yet were still connected to everything in much the same way the harp's music enveloped all the people in the music room last night. But there was something else, she thought. She shut her eyes, trying to remember. In the few brief moments she had played — those notes, the fragments of the harmony, the slips of melody were like remnants, shreds from a song she could almost recall.

A report came down from upstairs that a deal had been brokered between Lila and Mrs. Hawley. If Lila would cooperate with the requirements for the portrait, she could have an off-the-shoulder gown for her debut like the one she craved from the House of Worth. "All is well for now." Daze sighed as she sank down onto a kitchen stool, exhausted. "I tell you, that girl is the devil herself."

When Hannah had cleaned and prepared the drawing room, she had left the door that led off the back of the room open just a slot. She planned to take a peek when she could during the painting of the girls' portraits. Daze and Florrie and Roseanne were charged with preparing the girls in their portrait dresses. So Hannah had no chance of glimpsing them any other way.

Mr. Wheeler arrived at ten o'clock sharp. A servant of his had already delivered his easel and materials. It was not until almost eleven that Hannah was able to steal upstairs and peep through the crack in the door.

They were apparently having a break, and Ettie was regaling Mr. Wheeler with a story about how she had witnessed the birth of a baby elephant at the Paris zoo. There was much laughter and many giggles.

"Well, I didn't actually see *the* moment. But I was so happy Miss Ardmore was sick that day and Annabelle, our French parlor maid, took me."

"Annabelle used to dance in the Folies Bergère," Clarice added. "But don't tell Mummy or she could get fired and she's our favorite Paris maid."

"Anyway, Annabelle took me and it had just been born. They get born standing up."

"*No!*" Stannish Wheeler exclaimed.

"Well, not quite standing up," Clarice corrected. "I looked it up in the *Le Livre d'Histoire Naturelle des Animaux Exotiques*, and it said that within an hour of being born a baby elephant usually stands."

"But it still had some bloody stuff on it, and its belly button cord hanging down." Ettie spoke in a hushed awe.

Lila looked entirely bored. "Can we get back to the painting?" Lila yawned. "I have heard this elephant story a thousand times."

"No, you haven't," Ettie said staunchly. "Because nobody ever lets me tell it."

"Why is that, Ettie?" Mr. Wheeler asked as he crouched down and pulled at the hem of her skirt. Surreptitiously he slowly turned his head toward Hannah's door, and winked. Hannah felt the blood rush to her face and began to draw back, but he shook his head. The current had begun to flow again. She felt it. *He must have sensed me even before he saw me.*

"They say it's inappropriate to talk about such matters," Ettie replied to Mr. Wheeler's question. "But it's about getting born. I mean, if it's inappropriate to get born, where would we all be?" Hannah clapped a hand over her mouth to prevent herself from laughing out loud. She noticed that the corners of Mr. Wheeler's eyes crinkled up and there was a flash of white teeth. He looked at her again. There was something utterly delicious in sharing a joke in this clandestine way.

The painter had arranged the girls in an interesting tableau. Clarice and Ettie were in the foreground. Ettie was the closest but sitting on the floor. Her legs were straight out and she was holding one of her stuffed animals. Clarice was a few steps behind her, and then in the background Lila leaned languidly against an immense vase. Hannah almost experienced a feeling of envy as she saw that the top of Lila's head grazed that cresting wave from which the fish tail broke.

She knew it was silly. It was not as if Lila were in the sea. But in her casual posture she seemed to be claiming it in some way. She was the only one not facing the painter. All three girls were wearing rather young-looking frocks in shades of rose and lavender with fresh white pinafores. It was almost as if they were to be frozen in time at an age that represented the delicate cusp between little girl and young maiden. Hannah realized that she, too, was on this same edge, but how different her life was. She was expected to work and to learn how to negotiate the harsh realities of life.

The painting proceeded with the girls posing for the next few days. But there was a noticeable tension that had settled on number 18 Louisburg Square. It was as if the entire household was holding its breath . . . waiting . . . waiting, but Hannah was not sure exactly what for. Mr. and Mrs. Hawley would often drop their voices suddenly when servants entered the room. On the fifth morning after the painting had begun, Lila boldly sailed into the drawing room with Jade cradled in her arms.

Hannah crept back into the hallway, out of sight, but able to hear. Ettie's voice scratched the air with a slight whine that Hannah had never heard from her before.

"Lila, why'd you bring Jade?"

Hannah hated how Lila was standing there nuzzling the cat, so satisfied, so smug. Lila buried her nose in its thick white fur while the top of her head almost brushed the tail of the sea creature painted on the vase, the precise spot where Hannah had held up the tiny crystal to the teardrop-shaped scales. She actually had to push down an urge to rush out from behind the door and shove Lila away from the vase.

"You don't like cats, Mr. Wheeler?" asked Lila.

"Now, I never said that, Lila."

"You don't have to say it. I know it. It's against your nature. But natures can change."

He laughed nervously. "I'm sure I don't know what you're talking about."

"I'm sure you don't," Lila replied in a husky whisper.

Her words sent a chill through Hannah. It almost seemed like a threat.

"Mr. Wheeler doesn't have to paint Jade. I just want to hold my dear kitty." Lila paused. "It calms me," she said pointedly.

"My goodness, Lila. Why would a lovely young lady like yourself be agitated?" Mr. Wheeler asked.

"I don't know," Lila replied. "But many young ladies and older ones are afflicted by nerves, Mr. Wheeler. I have yearnings that cannot be fulfilled." She looked at him.

Yearnings? The word shot through Hannah like a bolt of lightning flaring within her with sizzling hot light. *What is she saying — yearnings? She has everything. Everything except him!*

Hannah heard Mr. Wheeler cough slightly. "Well, shall we get on with it, then?"

"My yearnings?" Lila's brittle laugh shattered the air. She posed with the cat the next day as well. The tension in the house increased. But in that moment Hannah realized that *yearnings* was the perfect word. She, too, yearned for something, but what exactly? The music she had so briefly played? Or was it what those fleeting notes that had spiraled into the night air represented, that elusive place where things moved freely?

Mr. and Mrs. Hawley continued their hectic social schedule with Lila and Clarice accompanying them to many concerts, teas, and the theater. There were more dinner parties as well, which they hosted at number 18. Lila attended these and perhaps to the guests she appeared quite normal. But her family and the servants knew she was wound as tight as a spring. They tiptoed around her. Mrs. Hawley made all sorts of concessions. Jade was now allowed to come to the breakfast and luncheon table.

Hannah tried to finish her upstairs tasks in Lila's bedroom quickly. She never again had a standoff with Jade as she had the first night. The cat seemed to know that she was the servant, who like Dotty before, brought milk and often thick cream. But Jade had a peculiar way of watching Hannah. And, oddly enough, when the cat watched her, it almost felt as if Lila were there.

⚜   ⚜   ⚜

The scullery maid was always the first up in the morning and the last to bed in the evening. There had been a great deal to clean up after that night's dinner party. It was well after midnight when Hannah made her way up the back stairs to her bedroom. The guttering flame in the oil lamp that she carried cast only the smallest pool of light, but when she arrived at her room, she froze in the open doorway and stifled a cry. Suspended in the darkness were two small iridescent slashes. Then a mound rose from her bed. Jade arched her back, her tail swooped up like a scimitar, her jaws dropped open revealing two curved white fangs, and her eyes fastened on that spot on Hannah's chest where the pouch rested beneath her dress. Hannah felt something seize within her. Her free hand automatically clutched at the pouch as a long hiss scalded the air. *She wants my pouch!* The thought streaked through Hannah's mind.

She lunged at the cat, her oil lamp swinging. Shadows danced off the wall. "Out! Out!" The cat darted from her bed and out of the room, swallowed up by the darkness of the hallway. Hannah stood motionless, her chest heaving, her heart pounding.

She lay rigid in her bed all night. From her window she watched the darkness wear to the dim gray of the dawn. And finally, long before she had to get up, she rose and began her morning activities. But all day long the sound of that hissing cat seemed to follow her through the house. The only place she did not hear it was in the music room. The instant she stepped into the lovely room that now spun with May sunlight, the liquid sounds of the harp came back to her. And each time she entered the room her fingers longed to touch those strings. Suddenly she was aware of someone watching her.

"Mr. Wheeler! Wh . . . wh . . . what are you doing here?"

"I might ask the same of you."

"I come here every day to lay the fire and dust."

"It's so warm. Is there really a need to come and build a fire on a lovely spring day like this?" Hannah didn't know what to say. He took a step forward. "I'll tell you what I think, Hannah." She started at the sound of her name. Guests in the house never knew the names of servants of her rank. "I think you long to play that harp."

"Why do you say that?" she asked in a trembling voice. He took a step closer to her. *I should move away but I can't,* she thought. *I can't. I won't. I don't want to.*

He was very close to her now. He picked up her hand and pressed it between his own cool hands. "I see music in you," he said simply. She stared at his fingers. She could see a remnant of paint near the cuticle of his thumb, a dark, purplish gray that he had used to make the shadows and to bring out the folds in the girls' dresses.

"You can't say these things," she said in a whispered voice. She felt the threat of tears, a hot, burning sensation beneath her cheekbones. Then the tears began to seep in a frail stream down her cheeks. He was drawing her closer. His face was very near hers. *He's going to kiss me.*

His lips brushed her cheek, which was wet now.

"There." When he stepped back, something sparkled on his lips. He released her hand and raised his fingers to his lips. A teardrop no longer liquid gleamed like the small ovals contained in the pouch Hannah wore. Taking her hand, the painter placed it gently in her palm. "Yours," he said quietly.

A shadow suddenly sliced across the puddle of sunlight by the door of the music room.

Hannah found that she could not resist the urge to watch the progress of the painting despite her vows to avoid Lila, Jade, and the painter as much as possible. So she took up her previous post in the narrow corridor by the door at the back of the drawing room. Through the slot she could see the girls arranging themselves. Once again Lila stood by the vase with the cat, which she now insisted on bringing, curled in her arms. Hannah wished that she had a better view of Mr. Wheeler's canvas. She wanted to see what he was seeing. How was he painting Lila? The vase? Jade? If he had seen music in her, what was he seeing in Lila? She had not been standing there long when for no reason at all Lila turned her head. The cat did as well. Hannah felt the glittering light of four hard gemstones drill into her. She slipped away from the door and pressed herself against the wall of the corridor.

Lunch for the servants was always an hour before the Hawleys'. When Hannah rushed in, Susie looked up. "Good gracious, Hannah! Looks like you've seen a ghost. Whatever is the matter?"

"It's Lila, Susie. I think . . . I think . . . she's after me."

"After you?" Susie's freckled face studied her for a few seconds. She put her hands on her broad hips. "Now, don't worry. She ain't after no one. She ain't got the wits."

"No!" Hannah said with such ferocity that Susie took a step back. "That's just where you're wrong. She does have the wits."

"Really, Hannah. She's got a very bad case of nerves. She's peculiar in the head and it makes . . ."

"No, Susie, listen to me. Lila is not simply peculiar in her head. She's got a weirdness of the heart, of the soul. She and that cat together." *Together* — the word had an odd ring for Hannah. "Together," did Lila and the cat recognize something in Hannah? Did they sense that Hannah herself felt incomplete? Or did they together want something that Hannah had? *But I have nothing, nothing at all.* Then she touched the cloth of her dress that covered the pouch. *Or is it this?* she wondered, and thought of the teardrop crystals enclosed in the grosgrain pouch.

Susie's lower lip started to tremble. "You scare me when you talk like this, Hannah."

"I am scared, Susie."

At the servants' lunch, Mr. Marston announced that preparations would begin for the family's transfer to Maine. "By the end of the week, Mr. Wheeler will have painted in enough that he can part with the vases. So they shall go in the first load."

Apparently it took two trips to transport the household of number 18 Louisburg Square to Maine. Gladrock was on the island of Mount Desert, which as Florrie had explained was not a "proper island" but connected by a causeway to the mainland. Hannah blessedly would go with the first contingent, which would travel there by steamer with the trunks and, of course, the vases. The thought of going to this not-proper island and living in a sprawling mansion, a mere five hundred feet from the sea, was the only thing that kept Hannah from quitting her job. But within the next two days she would be as severely tested as she had been during her month in Salina, Kansas.

Although Jade had not trespassed in Hannah's room again, Hannah always approached her with great caution. Hannah did not have a lock, since locks were forbidden by the Hawleys, but she had taken to latching her door firmly so it could not be pushed open by a stray breeze or a stray cat. However, the evening after the announcement of their upcoming departure for Maine, she experienced a sense of violation as soon as she walked into her room. Someone had been in the space. She looked about thoroughly, but none of her scant belongings had been disturbed.

She set the oil lamp by the bed and began to undress. She then went to her washstand, lit a second lamp, and poured water into the metal bowl to wash her face. Something swirled in the water, giving it a reddish tinge. When she bent over and looked closer, she saw small bits, like threads. Red threads. She turned around slowly and walked toward her bed with the lamp. On the pillow were other small filaments of red. She turned back the covers. More were scattered over the sheets. "My God," she whispered.

"Oh, dear, here's poor Dotty. Well, I guess that's you now. You don't mind, do you?" The conversation with Daze came back to Hannah from that day they had arranged the dollhouse. What Hannah was looking at was the hair that she and Daze had dyed with India ink.

Her breath locked in her throat. A fury rose in her. "Why me? What have I ever done to this hell hag and her hell cat?" She felt something harden in her. She would not be frightened. She might be a servant. She might have nothing. But she would not be cowed, bullied, intimidated by Lila Hawley. She gathered up as much as she could of the cut hair from the doll and folded it in a piece of writing paper. This was her evidence. Surely if Susie did not believe her, Daze would. But first she wanted to go to the nursery and see the doll. As she turned to leave, she noticed something she hadn't before. There was a small satin box with a pink ribbon tied around it by the baseboard next to the door frame. Crouching down, she picked it up and untied it. Inside was the upstairs maid costume in which she and Daze had dressed Hannah's doll. A tiny piece of paper lay on top of the miniature lilac dress with the ruffled apron and frilled mobcap. "Know your place, scullery girl."

Hannah stared at the box's contents for several minutes. Then, taking the box to the table by the washstand, she shook about half of the red threads into it. Very neatly she refolded the note and retied the bow. "We'll see who breaks first," Hannah muttered. And slipping the box into her pocket, she headed for the nursery.

"THAT DAMN CAT"

THE NEXT MORNING Hannah found Ettie in the nursery, kneeling in front of the dollhouse.

"Oh, no!" Ettie moaned.

"What is it, Ettie?" She thought for a moment that Ettie was about to discover what she had the night before — the Dotty figure with her hair shorn, her uniform changed, and hideous splotches painted on her face. But she had not found this at all.

"Look!" said Ettie, pointing toward the dollhouse room that was Lila's.

"What about it?" Hannah asked.

"See the bowl?"

"Jade's bowl?"

"Yes. She filled it with real milk." Ettie lifted her face toward Hannah. Fear flickered in her clear gray eyes. "Always a bad sign."

Hannah swallowed. "A bad sign?"

Ettie's brow furrowed as if she were thinking about the hardest thing imaginable. "I mean it seems that sometimes Lila loses her way" — she stopped — "or maybe it's Jade that loses her way. They go off together into this little world of their own and I think . . . I think, well, it's not so much who is pet and who is mistress, it's more like what is human and what is . . . is . . ."

"Animal?" Hannah whispered.

"Oh, no!" Ettie said defiantly. "It's an insult to all animals to consider Jade an animal, let alone a cat."

Hannah felt the color drain from her face. There was something so profoundly shocking about this small child's observations.

Ettie shook her head mournfully. "You'll see, you'll see," she said wearily as if it were beyond words to explain. "Better tell Mummy . . . no . . . no. Miss Ardmore, because if Mummy hears . . ." She never finished the sentence, and left the nursery to find Miss

Ardmore. Hannah watched her. Her little shoulders were rolled forward and hunched.

With the discovery of the milk in Jade's dollhouse bowl, things seemed to happen rapidly. Lila refused to come downstairs and the painting session was canceled for that morning. Hannah had been sent on some morning errands, but by the time she returned, it was like entering a house in a state of siege. Mr. Marston was holding forth in the kitchen. The dinner had been canceled for that evening. "But not the ladies' luncheon for tomorrow. No, Dr. Edwards is upstairs now administering a sedative. If the ladies' luncheon is canceled, Mrs. Hawley feels that talk will start and how right she is. Ladies do talk. We are to explain her absence this noon by saying that Lila has gone for a sail on the river with her cousin Harry and some of his young friends."

"More lying," Mrs. Bletchley muttered.

"All in a good cause, Mrs. Bletchley," Mr. Marston replied.

Good cause! thought Hannah. Lila was hardly a

good cause. It must be the family's reputation they feared for. Even Hannah knew what the taint of madness did to a young woman's marriage prospects.

"What about going to Gladrock, Mr. Marston?" Miss Horton asked. "How does this affect our schedule?"

"If anything, I think it might accelerate it."

Hannah felt a stir of excitement. If she could just get to this not-quite-proper island by the sea, she felt she could endure anything. "Is there anything I can do, Mr. Marston," Hannah asked, "to help . . . ?" She paused. "Accelerate things for going to Gladrock?"

"How very kind of you, Hannah." He looked up at her brightly. A smile creased his face. It was the first time anybody had smiled all morning. "Let me say, Hannah, that Mr. and Mrs. Hawley have been most impressed with the few times you have served at their more formal dinner parties, and I feel that, God willing, if Lila improves, there will be more occasions at Gladrock for you to serve. But, yes, back to the subject. I suppose it might be helpful if you could begin packing up the dollhouse in the nursery. That always takes a bit of time, doesn't it?"

Something wilted in Hannah at the mention of the dollhouse. Of all the tasks to be given! But she pushed such thoughts out of her mind. She wanted to get to Maine as fast as possible. "Yes, Mr. Marston. I'll be pleased. Of course."

Somehow Hannah felt that if she were near the sea, really close to it, she could endure Lila. Once again she touched the pouch beneath her dress and thought of the teardrop crystals so like those scales of the painted creature on the vase.

"What in the world happened to you?" Daze asked as she started to slip the dollhouse figure of the scullery girl into the servants' shoe box. "Have you seen this, Hannah?" She held up the figure.

"Yes, unfortunately. The hair that was cut was left in my bedroom."

"What?" Daze gasped. Hannah nodded. "Do you think it was Lila?"

"I doubt it was Ettie or Clarice," Hannah replied in an expressionless voice.

Daze's eyes hardened. Her lips pressed into a grim little line. "I really hate her. She might be crazy but she's mean. Crazy mean. Look how we're all tiptoeing around. Poor Ettie was in tears this morning."

"So what are we supposed to do now about Lila's dollhouse room? She's hardly in shape to get up and put the stuff in its box herself. How do we pack it up if we're not allowed to touch it?" Hannah asked.

Daze cocked her chin defiantly. "It's a dollhouse, for the love of God. She might be the tail that wags the dog in number Eighteen, but Mr. Marston told us to pack it up and that is exactly what we are going to do." She began removing the tiny furnishings from Lila's dollhouse room, wrapping them in tissue, and putting them in the box labeled LILA'S BEDROOM. Hannah had never realized what a feisty spirit Daze was. She had always thought of her as a rather pliant girl, quiet and rarely showing anger even when Miss Horton reprimanded her for not dusting properly. Miss Horton seemed to criticize Daze quite a bit for no good reason at all. But it was apparent that when truly provoked, Daze could be roused.

"Here's Jade," Hannah said, picking up the white porcelain cat, and began rolling it in cotton and then in the tissue paper.

"Now I know which cat they were talking about when they first said 'mean as cat's piss,'" Daze said and flung the creature into the box after Hannah handed it to her.

The next morning Hannah was in the kitchen, peeling potatoes with Susie, when a terrible screeching was heard, followed by thumps. Mr. Marston immediately set down the paper he had been reading and raced upstairs. He returned in a few minutes, pale, his eyes darting with near terror. "Jade has gone missing! She must have slipped out. Miss Lila is in a state. She hit Ettie, who is bleeding. What are you all standing there for?" he roared.

"But what are we to do?" Mrs. Bletchley said in a shrill voice.

"Start looking for the damn cat!" Susie, Hannah, and Mrs. Bletchley looked at one another in stunned amazement. Never had they heard Mr. Marston use an oath. Then, caught up by his own profanity, he coughed slightly and adjusted his tie. "Pardon me, Mrs. Bletchley."

"Don't worry, sir."

"You did wrap up the fish trimmings and the bones from last night's dinner, didn't you, good and tight?" Mr. Marston asked.

"Oh, of course, sir. I always do. But I can't count on the neighbors. If the Bennetts' cook didn't . . . Well . . . you know how that cat goes crazy over fish."

Susie sidled up to Hannah and whispered, "Last year she ate every fish in the Waltons' garden pond down the block. Every last one, except the one Willy found her playing with. It was still alive! He said it was disgusting. She was sporting with it, before she bit its head off."

Mrs. Bletchley made a *tsk*ing sound and calmly went back to carving a radish with a paring knife into the shape of a tulip. Daze came rushing into the kitchen. "I've already looked all over the upstairs. We'll have to get Willy to crawl out on the roof."

Mrs. Bletchley kept her eyes on the radish and said in a dark, menacing voice, "If that sweet boy falls off the roof for that damn cat, I'll skin the creature alive and cook her up for Lila." This time no looks were exchanged and no one waited for Mrs. Bletchley to apologize for her profanity.

⚜　⚜　⚜

"She's what?" Susie and Hannah both wheeled around as Florrie came running into the kitchen.

"Lila has accused Mr. Wheeler of murdering the cat."

"Have they found the cat?"

"No. She just said he did it. He didn't like the cat in the picture. Therefore he killed Jade." Mr. Marston then came in a minute later. "This talk will go no further than the kitchen."

"It's not true, is it, Mr. Marston?" Susie asked.

"Of course it's not true, Susie. Lila Hawley is a deeply disturbed young woman. The specialist who visited this afternoon has made a diagnosis of acute neurasthenia. She will be leaving within three hours for Foxcroft to take a rest cure. Daze, Susie, and Hannah, you should prepare to leave within two days for Gladrock. Reservations have been made on the coastal steamer *Elizabeth M. Prouty*. She's of the Kennebec Steamboat Company. So that means she will be departing from Lincoln Wharf at ten o'clock sharp."

Hannah could hardly believe her ears. *I am going to sea! Going to sea. To an island — proper or not — in the sea!* Hannah remembered that Daze had once said that the vases looked better at Gladrock than anywhere else. She had a sudden urge to go see them. There was no one in the drawing room at the moment. *Why not?* she thought.

The windows were wide open in the drawing room, for the weather was fine and Miss Horton had an obsession about "airing" rooms on fine days. The sun slid through the tall French windows and laid a bright rectangular plank of light on the polished floor. There was a whiter-than-white flash against the rectangle of sunlight. Hannah's eyes flinched. It was as if something unconscious had been torn from her mind, from her imagination, and become real. *No, it can't be.* At the very center of her denial was dread, for despite the airing, a distinct, rank odor slid through the air like a thin ribbon. *A cat has been here.* Hannah walked as if in a trance toward the vase on the right, closest to the window. The scent became stronger. There was a wet patch on the surface of the vase just where the fish creature's tail broke through the waves.

"Mr. Marston!" Hannah cried out. "Mr. Marston!"

Mr. Marston arrived with Florrie. It didn't take long to search the room and establish that Jade was nowhere about, but there was absolutely no doubt that she had been minutes before. Miss Horton was called. When she entered, her thin face flinched and the tip of that long pointy nose appeared to take on a life of its own. She walked straight to the vase. "Unbelievable!" she exclaimed.

"I am afraid it is quite believable, Miss Horton," Mr. Marston said, touching his nose lightly.

"Yes," she said, turning to the butler. "Figures of speech no longer suffice."

"It's a defilement," Mr. Marston said.

"Filth is what it is!" she snapped. "Have you checked inside?"

Hannah saw Mr. Marston's lips move but no sound came. He tried again. "Inside, Miss Horton. Inside what?"

"Inside the vase."

"For . . . for . . ." Mr. Marston hesitated. "Droppings?" Mr. Marston turned deathly pale, his skin more bleached than Miss Horton's scrubbed countenance. "Surely, Miss Horton, I can't imagine . . ."

"You can't imagine, but I can," she replied. Mr. Marston seemed to waver slightly as he stood there. For a moment Hannah thought he might actually faint.

"Fetch a stepladder, Hannah," Miss Horton ordered. "And, Florrie, I believe a small torch lamp and also a solution: one part carbolic acid to eight parts water, one quarter cup Javelle cleanser, one quarter cup chloride of lime. You have that?"

"Yes, ma'am!"

Five minutes later Hannah was peering into the vase. She had lowered on a rope a small kerosene lantern that illuminated the interior of the vase. She felt a wave of relief flow through her when she saw nothing in the bottom of the vase. Hannah realized that the shape of the vase was as lovely on the inside as on the out. She felt a warm surge within her. She whispered into the contoured half-light of the vase, "We are going home — home," and she touched the pouch with its teardrop crystals.

"Hannah, what do you see? Anything?" The authoritative timbre of Mr. Marston's voice had been restored.

"Nothing, sir. Nothing at all."

"No stench?" Miss Horton called up.

"Oh, no . . . not a whiff of anything."

"Well," Mr. Marston began, "the Japanese ceramics were fired at very high temperatures, making them impervious to fluids . . ." But as Mr. Marston gave a lecture on the porcelains from Kyoto, Hannah did catch a scent — the clear tang of a salt breeze coming off the sea. *This vase contains a world — another world!* Hannah was suddenly aware of a cool glow radiating from the pouch and an odd stirring in her feet.

For the rest of the day and into the evening, the odd sensation in Hannah's feet seemed to creep up toward her ankles. Sometimes it felt like a delicate stirring, and at other times it was almost like a whisper, a liquid murmur. It did not interfere with her walking. If anything, she felt as if she were gliding just slightly above the polished wood floors and Oriental carpets of number 18. And despite the general uproar of the house over the missing cat, Hannah experienced a sense of calm and freedom. It was as if Jade's disappearance brought a new serenity within herself and a newfound grace. She could not wait until her chores for the day were finished. It was Hannah's turn to bathe first in the old cast-iron claw-footed tub that the serving girls shared, and she wanted to examine her feet.

Finally, at the end of the day, Hannah was alone in the water closet. The space was a stark one, with the slipper-shaped old tub and its lion-claw feet taking up the scant room. There was a single hook on which to hang one's uniform and a small stool to place a bath towel. Hannah began to undress. She always removed the grosgrain pouch last. The pouch now contained the teardrop she had shed in the music room that had been mysteriously transformed on the painter's lips into an iridescent oval like the others.

When she undressed she usually tucked the pouch into the deepest pocket of her dress. But tonight there was a slight alteration of her ritual. She took her pouch off first and did not tuck it away into the pocket. She could still feel the radiant spot on her chest as she opened the pouch. She peered in and gasped. She could see nothing but a luminous mist in the pouch. Panic seized her. Had the teardrop crystals dissolved, leaving only this cool vapor behind, like a last breath of some sort? Then once more she felt that whispering around her feet and quickly peeled off her stockings.

At first glance her feet and ankles looked as they always had — pale, slender with blue veins that crossed over the top and slanted toward her ankle bone beneath the white, nearly translucent skin. But

then she spied something else. A netting, a fine filigree, was dimly visible. She bent closer. The pattern
of the netting resembled lace, but the open-
ings were not mere circles or diamonds. They were
teardrops!

"What has happened here?" Hannah whispered as
she looked at her feet and ran her hands over them.
She opened the pouch again and peered in. The
mist was still contained, but she could discern a
few crystals — quite ordinary-looking actually, with
none of the luminous glow of the vapor that surrounded them.

Twenty minutes later, after she had taken her
bath and gone to bed, there was a soft rapping on
her door.

"Yes."

"It's me, Florrie. Don't mean to disturb you."

"What is it?"

"Well, Daze and I are itching like crazy and the tub
smells of salt — not those fancy kinds of bath salts
that the Hawley girls use. Something stronger. Are
you itching, too?"

"Uh . . . I didn't use any bath salts." Hannah shut her eyes tight and lied. "But, yes, I am itching. I wonder if somehow when the tub was cleaned, we didn't dilute the borax and Javelle solution enough."

"That's probably it," Florrie replied.

"Yes, probably." But Hannah vowed that she would never again bathe first.

BEYOND WORDS

THE *ELIZABETH M. PROUTY* steamed out of Boston Harbor and angled north and east across Massachusetts Bay. As soon as they rounded Cape Ann, billowing seas rolled in from the east. "Oh, dear!" Susie sighed.

"What's wrong?" Hannah turned to look at her. They were standing together on the deck.

"It always gets me when we round Cape Ann. It's like the whole ocean comes swirling in, stirring up my innards." A gray tinge had crept beneath Susie's usually rosy complexion, draining her of color. "That's open sea out there. The whole Atlantic," she whispered.

Hannah was ecstatic at the view that so frightened Susie. But she was careful to conceal her enthusiasm.

Since the evening before when she had bathed and discovered that filigree of teardrop lace, she had realized that a very strange shift had begun deep within her. She had checked her feet at least a half a dozen times since bathing. The change in them seemed to depend on the time of the day — sometimes it was more visible than others. But perhaps the strangest thing of all for Hannah was that although she felt herself moving away from all the things that she had once longed for, those things that would make her feel "fit and proper," it no longer disturbed her. She felt that she was going toward something new, that she was on the brink of something a little bit frightening but at the same time, true.

She closed her eyes and let the rhythms of the sea wrap around her. It was not unlike the night that she first felt the vibrations of the harp strings traveling up through the din of the nor'easter to her bed. Now there was not a storm, but the roar of the steamship's engines and the crushing sound of its prow slicing through the waves. Nonetheless Hannah was able to tease out the deeper rhythms and melodies of the sea that resonated like the music of the harp, but even more powerfully. And in that moment she knew that she could not only play the harp, but if she were swept from this deck into the sea, she could swim as well.

Deep within her soul, in her spirit, in her very muscle was an ancient music that sang like a memory as old as all the oceans. She would have to be patient, but she burned to know what was happening to her. She sensed that the painter knew. He was also part of this world, or he had been at some time. Of this, too, she was certain.

Before they had rounded the jutting cape, the air had been punctuated by the clanging of the occasional bell buoy or the mournful groan of a whistle buoy exhaling into the mist. But finally the coastline slipped away completely. They were truly on the open sea. Not a speck of land would be visible until much later that night, and only if the sky cleared and the moon and the stars were visible.

Hannah felt a strange and wonderful peace fill her, a harmony surging through the deepest recesses of her mind. She never went below to the tiny cabin that she shared with Daze and Susie and two serving girls from other Boston families. She stayed out all day and all through the night. The fog cleared, the stars broke out, and a slice of moon sailed high in the sky. On the horizon, she saw a mound rising from the sea. She walked forward to the bow rail. The sky at this time of night appeared not black but almost dark blue, with the sea gray against it.

"That be Isle au Haut," said Sal, the friendly crew member who had been answering all her questions. "And you see that flickering to starboard?" Hannah squinted. She glimpsed something that appeared like a firefly popping up and down behind the horizon line.

"Yes, yes! I see it."

"That's the Mount Desert Rock Lighthouse. It be twenty miles or so south of Mount Desert Island."

The night became a deeply radiant blue and within another few minutes a profile reared up from the sea.

"Green Mountain," Sal said.

"And it's on Mount Desert?" Hannah asked. "A mountain on a mountain!" She laughed.

"Yes, that's Mount Desert. And that's her mountain." *And that*, Hannah thought happily, *is the almost-proper island and I am going there!*

Other islands and lighthouses began to appear like sentries along the sea path to Mount Desert. There was Long Island, the Cranberries, Great Duck Light, Baker Island Light. Most of these were given a wide berth as the *Elizabeth M. Prouty* plied the now-smooth waters. They skimmed by one lighthouse island as they turned to port and entered Frenchman Bay. It was the last lighthouse before they landed, called Egg Rock Light.

They came so close, Hannah felt she could almost reach out and touch it. Built on a rocky ledge to mark the entrance to the bay, it was a homely lighthouse set in a half-story building, stolid and square with worn clapboards. A dormer projected from each of the four sides of the roof like a blunt beak. In the center of the building, an ungainly brick tower rose, which held the light. The island on which the house perched like a squat, flightless bird with its beak to the wind was scoured by the sea. There was hardly a blade of grass, but the granite rocks sloped gently into the water.

As they sailed by, Hannah caught a glimpse of a girl standing at the edge of one rock looking longingly at the horizon. Hannah inhaled sharply. It was almost as if she were seeing a mirror image of herself. The girl was the same height and had a willowy build that seemed to bend into the breeze. But mostly it was the way the sunlight caught the girl's hair. It was just after dawn and the reddish tones of her hair sparkled and seemed touched by a delicate greenish cast. In another few minutes the sun would be higher and Hannah knew that the girl's long, blowing curls would erupt in a dazzling conflagration of red flames. She felt something quicken inside her.

☙ ❧   ☙ ❧   ☙ ❧

It was all hustle and bustle as soon as they walked down the gangplank. It seemed as if the entire population had come to greet the *Elizabeth M. Prouty*. In the midst of the crowd a small bowlegged man was waving his cap and shouting, "Daze! Daze!"

"It's my dad!" Daze exclaimed. And suddenly Hannah realized that indeed Daze's peculiar accent was neither peculiar nor unique here. Everyone was speaking in those funny swooping rhythms, then chopping off the sound abruptly. And instead of saying yes, the word was *a-yuh*.

"This is Hannah, Dad."

"A-yuh."

"She's ever so clever, and is really becoming more of an upstairs maid than just a scullery girl."

"A-yuh."

"And Susie came with us, and Willy, and the vases, of course."

"A-yuh."

And so it went. Daze's father, Perl, was the grounds-keeper and general handyman for Gladrock. He had brought with him two buckboards and three men to help with the loading of the vases, the dollhouse, and the steamer trunks of the Hawleys.

"We walk," Daze explained. "It ain't far at all."

They followed a road through the village of Bar Harbor, which only consisted of the one main street, two hotels, a few cottages, and three churches. The wharves were piled high with lobster traps, and bobbing just off the wharves were dozens of skiffs, dories, sloops, and schooners with faded sails, many patched from old clothes. The strong scent of fish pervaded everything, and Hannah noticed mounds of cod left to dry in the sun. The air seemed to have a special brilliance on this morning, and Hannah gasped as they rounded each bend and saw a new finger of land stretching out into the bay.

Just on the edge of town they passed a general store called Bee's.

"Oh!" exclaimed Susie. "We have to go in and buy some penny candy. They have the best penny candy here. And the chocolate drops are heaven."

The three girls went into the store. It was crowded with people and Hannah noticed that not only did the people say a-yuh quite a bit, but everyone — from the first meeting — addressed females as "dear."

With the Maine accent the word was broken into almost two syllables and became *de-ah*.

Daze and Susie advised Hannah on what to buy. Hannah could not believe one little store could hold so much. In addition to candy and fresh vegetables — the first of the season — there were fancy cookies, pastries, writing paper and pens, mousetraps, oil for lamps, candles, beeswax, and honeycombs fresh from the hive. The store was filled now with "natives." Daze had been quick to explain the different classes of people on Mount Desert. The natives were people like her dad and herself who had been born and raised on the island. The natives could now be heard discussing the "rusticators." That was the term used for all the summer people, but not their servants, who were just called servants. But the rusticators were divided into the "mealers," who rented houses and lived near enough to hotels to walk to the dining rooms, and the "hauled mealers," who had to be driven in buckboards or pony traps because the distance was too far to walk. And then there were the "cottagers," or summer people like the Hawleys who owned their own houses and had a staff of servants to cook, serve meals, captain their sailing yachts, take care of their gardens, and do anything else that might add to their summer enjoyment for the two or three months they spent on this not-proper island. The natives of Mount Desert were by and large fishermen. They fished for anything that swam in the sea, trapped lobsters, and dug in the mud flats for clams. They were rugged men and women. Many of the women served in the hotels and the cottages of the rusticators during the summer, as did their children and some of the men who no longer fished.

About ten minutes after the girls had left Bee's, they turned into a wooded lane that dipped and wound through a pine and balsam forest. Hannah thought she had never smelled anything lovelier than the scent of salt air mingling with the tangy pungency of these trees. The path was covered with a thick layer of pine needles that muffled their footsteps and even softened the sound of voices. The lane then became more of a drive, which was composed of crushed shells — pinky orange ones of lobsters, purple mussel shells, and weathered clams.

Suddenly a great, sprawling, gray-shingled house rose up from the greenest lawn Hannah had ever seen.

"A cottage!" Hannah exclaimed. "You call this a cottage? I've never seen anything bigger in my life."

"I know," said Susie. "The rich folks up here call their houses cottages for some reason. I'm not sure why. Maybe they think it makes them fit in somehow with the natives."

"Just how would that be?" Hannah asked, almost laughing out loud.

The three girls made their way across the lush lawn. All around the house dozens of servants were scurrying about. Men were walking with two-wheeled carts, spreading something on the flower beds. Others were raking the lawn, some were clipping the hedges. As they walked up to the front door, two maids came running out. "Daze! Susie!" they called.

"We aren't going in through the front door, are we?" Hannah asked.

"Oh, yes, the Hawleys won't be here for a week. We can come and go as we please until then."

But Hannah hardly heard, for she had just

caught sight of the sea. She began to run across the lawn toward the water. Then she stopped stock-still. This was beyond her wildest dreams. Across a small sloping meadow there was the water, less than five hundred feet from the front door. The water nestled into a snug cove that opened onto Frenchman Bay and gave a view of Egg Rock Lighthouse and the islands beyond. Beyond that was the sea, the vast sea for thousands upon thousands of miles.

⚜   ⚜   ⚜

The next seven days were the happiest days Hannah had ever known. The bedroom she shared with Susie and Daze was tucked away high in the eaves of the house. Her bed was in a narrow dormer with a small round window that framed a piece of the water, two dark spruce trees, and a lavender rock that slanted into the sea. That was all she needed. Anytime she looked through the window, Hannah glimpsed the endlessly changing moods of the sea. All through the night she could hear its distant surge against the outer rocks and imagine the cresting waves she could not quite see.

All day she worked hard alongside Daze, Susie, and half a dozen island girls to get the house ready for the Hawleys. But in the early evenings, she would go down to the slanting rock and sit silently. Some days the fog was thick. "Thick as mud," Daze's father would announce when he came into the kitchen at six in the morning for his mug of coffee.

One evening, a few days before the family's arrival, all the servants went into the village for a dance at the church hall. The natives' church, not the fancier one where the rusticators went. Hannah had no desire to go. She much preferred to stay right at Gladrock and perhaps go down to her own "glad rock," as she now thought of the lavender stone, which was much smaller than the huge granite expanse that the "cottage" was named for. She just had a bit more sewing to do on Ettie's summer clothes and her bathing costume, which intrigued Hannah to no end. Ettie apparently was the only one of all the Hawleys who dared swim in the frigid Maine waters and she was only permitted to do this under the strict supervision of adults. Most of the rusticators, and especially the cottagers, swam at the swank tennis and swimming club in the saltwater swimming pool. But not Ettie.

Hannah wondered how in the world one ever managed to swim in such a costume. Made of wool, the outfit consisted of three-quarter-length trousers and a belted jacket. Beneath the trousers were striped stockings and then there were special lace-up bathing shoes. When she had finished stitching the hems on the trousers, which had to be let down two inches since Ettie had shot up quite a bit since the previous summer, Hannah thought she would go down to the cove and her rock. As she came down the stairs, she noticed that a door to a room she had not yet been in had been left partway open. She gently pushed open the door and walked in.

"Oh!" Hannah said softly. A harp stood by a tall window, illuminated by a stream of moonlight. This time there was not a soul in the entire house — no servant, no family, no Jade. The harp beckoned Hannah, just as the moon lures the tides. For only the second time in her life she eased a harp onto her shoulder. As soon as it touched, an energy coursed through her. She did not even think of the woman who played that night when she first heard the music. Her own fingers fell naturally on the strings. There was again a remnant torn from some ancient fabric, a memory of music that came to her as she began to play the strings.

A series of notes issued into the night and were suspended in the air, like bubbles, like silver drops of moonlight. Was it water or was it light? She had played those notes with her right hand but now tried it with her left, placing her fingers in a different position on the strings. The tones were deeper, darker, richer, but when she combined them with the ones she had coaxed from the strings with her right hand, a soft illumination seemed to suffuse the sound.

The seconds stretched into minutes. There were no interruptions.

It all came to her instinctively. Hannah did not know the names of the notes that her fingers brought forth. She did not know that for the first several minutes she had been exploring the scales, an arrangement of notes in an ascending and descending order of pitch, or that the striking difference she discovered between the intervals of notes in which sometimes the vibrations seemed to multiply and at other times diminish was a musical phenomenon known as an octave. She just felt it, just did it.

She would no more have questioned her ability to play than she would her capacity to breathe. It did not seem in the least extraordinary; it seemed natural. Once more she had the feeling that as the mystery deepened, she was moving toward a more profound truth. Hannah played late into the night, until she heard the laughter of the servants returning from the village. There would be other times when she played the harp. And although she did not know it at the time, she would later think of this night as the first in her transformation.

"DON'T OR CAN'T?"

TWO DAYS LATER the Hawleys arrived. Even though Hannah and the other servants could not come and go through the front door of Gladrock, were required to use the back stairs, and had much more work, it did not matter to Hannah. She would not be able to play the harp, but still she had her little bed tucked under the eaves with its round window that gave her a view of the sea.

During the first two weeks after the Hawleys arrived, it seemed as if there were nonstop parties. The entertainment was quite different from that in Boston. There were picnics almost every day and tennis and croquet parties. The household seemed happy and relaxed and completely free of the tension that had gripped it throughout most of the spring. There was absolutely no mention made of Lila.

Ettie drove Miss Ardmore ragged, for there was no keeping up with the child. She was, as her father said, "in her element in Maine." One minute she was in the vegetable garden helping one of the ten gardeners weed. The next she was clambering into her bathing costume and asking someone to watch her while she swam. A frequently heard phrase around Gladrock was, "Is there a grown-up around to guard my life?"

One day while Hannah was helping to serve breakfast, Ettie came running into the breakfast room barefoot in her bathing costume. "The tide is perfect for finding sand dollars. Perl is putting lobster crates on the mooring to keep them fresh for tonight's party. Does he count as a responsible adult for guarding my life?"

"Well, he's certainly an adult," Horace Hawley said, laughing. "Pushing seventy, I'd say. Is that right, Daze?" Daze was pouring coffee.

"No, sir, more like sixty. But that's the way it is downeast." *Downeast* was the natives' word for Maine.

"And he's responsible," Mrs. Hawley said. "But if he's busy with the lobsters, how can he watch you, too? And we must have all those lobsters because Mr. Wheeler arrives today and we promised." Hannah caught her breath. *He was coming today!*

"I could watch her, ma'am," Hannah offered.

"Can you swim?" Mr. Hawley asked.

"Oh, yes, sir," Hannah answered immediately. It wasn't a lie. She knew it was true. She knew that although she had never gone swimming before, it would be like the harp strings she had never touched until two weeks ago. She would simply do it. Somewhere within her there was this knowledge, *this . . . this . . . this gift*, she thought.

So Hannah accompanied Ettie down to the cove beach. Daze's father, Perl, was perhaps thirty feet off the beach in a dory, wrestling with the "lobster car," a slatted wooden box in which the lobsters were kept tethered to a mooring until they would be fetched to boil for that evening's "lobster feed."

"Hi, Perl!" Ettie yelled. "I have two responsible adults here. I'm going swimming."

"All right, de-ah. You do that. I'll fish you out with this grappling hook if you start to sink." He held up a line with a large hook on it.

"Yeah, and put me in the pot with the lobsters." Ettie laughed. She bent over and picked up a rock. "Have you ever seen me skip stones, Hannah?"

"No, I can't say as I have."

"I'm very good. You have to find the right stone. They have to be flat and not too big. Here's one." She bent over and picked it up. Holding it, she turned her palm up and with a quick motion swept her hand toward the water. The pebble released and skipped twice.

"Very good!" Hannah exclaimed.

"I can make it skip three times."

"Why don't you get in the water," Hannah urged. "The tide's going out. It won't be deep enough to swim."

"Just one more thing I've got to show you," replied Ettie.

"What's that?"

"I'm also very good at throwing rocks and hitting a target. Watch this. See that sea lavender? I call it sea violets, though."

"Yes," Hannah replied.

There was a spray of pale purple flowers on silvery stems growing out of the pebbly beach of the cove, thirty feet from where they stood. "Now watch this. I can hit those violets." Ettie picked up a good-size rock and swung her arm around like a pitcher winding up. The rock sailed into the air and landed smack in the plant. The tiny blossoms trembled.

"Hope you didn't hurt the plant. They are so pretty."

"Oh, no, they're very tough. They can stand the salt, the water coming in and out. That one probably gets covered at high tide. Here, let me pick you some." Ettie scampered over, bent down, and snapped off a few stems, then brought them back to Hannah.

She curtseyed and held out her hand with the flowers. "For you!" Ettie looked up shyly.

"Thank you." Hannah curtseyed back. "Now, are you ever going to get into that water?"

"Yes, right now," Ettie replied and walked toward the lapping waves.

Hannah felt the excitement growing in her. She had never before seen anyone really swimming. She had seen pictures in books, drawings, engravings, paintings of children swimming in ponds or splashing in the surf, but never in real life had she seen a human being immersed in the water. The stirrings that she felt in her feet intensified and crept up her legs. She had once thought of the sensation as a liquid murmur, but now there was a pulse, flickering in her bones. The cool radiance from the pouch seemed to spread throughout her body.

"Whooo-eee! It's cold this morning!" Ettie shrieked as she waded into the water. "Oh, I forgot my swimming booties. Oh, well. Now you count to three, Hannah, and then I'll plunge in."

"All right." Hannah laughed. "One-two-three."

Ettie looked around and smiled, slightly embarrassed. "Uh, count to, say, eight."

"Okay, here we go." Hannah began to count. She reached five and saw Ettie looking at her nervously. "Six, seven . . . seven and a half . . . eight." *Will she plunge in? It must be awfully cold*, Hannah thought.

"Eeeoow!" Ettie flung up her arms and rushed into the water. There was a ferocious splashing and water spangled the sunlit air.

Hannah watched mesmerized as Ettie ducked under, then came up again. "It's really nice once you get used to it," she yelled.

Every fiber in Hannah's body longed to be where Ettie was and yet she knew intuitively that this was not the time. Perhaps like the first time with the harp when a single strain of a vibration sought her, she would be called, summoned, gathered to the water. She was not yet ready. But she would be. Her season was coming; of this she was certain.

❧   ❧   ❧

Ettie didn't exactly swim, although Hannah had no doubt that she could. The little girl seemed quite buoyant, but she more or less jumped about, ducking and splashing, rolling herself in a little ball, trying to do an underwater somersault, and then every few seconds calling out, "Watch this, Hannah!" or "Look at this. I invented this trick myself." The cumbersome bathing costume did not seem to impede her at all.

She was in the water for almost half an hour, and when she emerged, her lips were blue and her teeth chattering. Hannah wrapped her in a big fleecy towel. "Now come on, Ettie. We have to run up to the house. Your mother and Miss Ardmore made me promise I'd get you up there as soon as you came out. And you have to go to Helen Beaton's birthday party."

"She's so stupid."

"What an unkind thing to say, Ettie. I've never heard you say anything unkind like that before."

"Well, she's not stupid, but her birthday party always is."

"Why's that?"

"Oh, we have to wear party dresses and play dumb games."

"What's dumb about the games?"

"They're girl games so you won't mess up your party dresses. So boring. My birthday is in winter, but if I had a summer birthday, I'd have a swimming party." Ettie's voice came out all shivery for she was still shaking with cold. "As a matter of fact, I think I might change my birthday. Oh, yes! What a fantastic idea. My real birthday is December twentieth. Stupid time for a birthday. Too close to Christmas. I think I'll change it. Let's see . . . maybe August fifteenth, that's not far off at all. The water will be even warmer. And not only that, it's during the nights of the shooting stars."

"The shooting stars?" Hannah asked.

"Oh, yes!" Ettie clapped her hands together. "It's the most beautiful time. The stars start to fall from the sky. That's it! I'm going to have a nighttime swimming and shooting stars party. We'll float on our backs and watch the sky. And we'll have games. Whoever sees the most falling stars wins. Oh, I'm so excited, I don't know how I never thought of this before. Quick! I've got to go talk to Daddy!" She scampered up through the meadow and onto the lawn.

"Ettie, wait up!" Hannah called, running after her. She could just imagine Ettie racing into her father's study dripping wet.

An immense oak spread its shade along the entire front of the porch. Clarice was reading under it as she often did. She looked up from her book now as Ettie rushed close by her, dropping her damp towel.

"Don't drop your old wet, salty towel on my books," Clarice said crossly. "Honestly." Clarice sighed, then muttered, "One sister's a loon and another half seal. Veritable menagerie here."

"Sorry," Ettie said with barely a glance and rushed up the porch stairs, followed by Hannah, who picked up the towel. When Hannah rose up she saw that another figure had just stepped onto the porch from the main house. *The painter!* He stood back in the shadows and watched as Hannah approached.

Hannah came onto the porch and put the towel around Ettie's shoulders, then shrank back so that she was out of the painter's line of vision. It was too disconcerting to see him in front of all these people. She had not seen him since he kissed her in the music room. Thankfully Ettie soon became the center of attention.

"Mummy! I want to change my birthday to August fifteenth, and we'll have a swimming party. I want to check the tide tables to make sure that there'll be enough water for night swimming, because we'll want to see the stars, too."

"Ettie! For heaven's sakes, you're dripping all over and can't you even say hello to Mr. Wheeler?"

"Hello!" Ettie looked up, still shivering.

"My goodness, you look charming all wet and fresh from the sea. A sea creature. Maybe I should paint you swimming?"

"Oh, Stannish, don't be ridiculous!" Mrs. Hawley laughed.

"It's a wonderful idea!" Ettie exclaimed. "You could paint me doing my water tricks. I've nearly perfected the underwater somersault."

"But how would I paint you if you are underwater the whole time?" the painter asked.

"Not the whole time," Ettie replied. "And maybe you could come in the water and see me when I was under, then run to the beach and sketch a little, then back into the water." Hannah now turned her head and observed the painter boldly. She felt her heart race. *Don't lie!* a voice in her head suddenly commanded. *Don't!*

"But, Ettie, I don't swim," the painter replied.

"Don't swim?" Ettie said, astounded. Her teeth had finally stopped chattering. She cocked her head and said, "Don't or can't swim, Mr. Wheeler?"

"Ettie!" Mrs. Hawley gasped. "Don't be pert now."

"Can't, Ettie," the painter replied simply. And although the remark was directed at Ettie, Mr. Wheeler dipped his chin and this time turned his eyes toward Hannah as he spoke. Hannah was shocked. There was alarming wretchedness etched in every line in his face. She had never seen such profound sorrow. She averted her eyes, wondering if anyone else noticed it. But they all seemed completely oblivious.

"Now, Hannah, please take Ettie upstairs," Mrs. Hawley said. "And will you come back down, Hannah? I have something I want to ask you."

"Yes, ma'am," Hannah replied.

GIRL IN THE SHADOWS

"**But I don't understand,** ma'am," Hannah protested. "I mean the portrait was being painted in Boston in the drawing room and everything is so different here." Mrs. Hawley looked at Stannish Wheeler, who took a few steps closer to Hannah. *Please don't come any closer*, Hannah prayed silently. *Whatever are you trying to do?*

"Yes, Hannah, I understand your concern." He made it somehow sound personal, but she cared not a whit one way or the other. She just didn't understand how it could be done. "You see," he continued, "the general background of the painting has been completed. And so has, for that matter, the foreground with Clarice and Ettie. Lila is in the background where there are more shadows and her figure is not . . ." He hesitated. "So distinct."

"But still, I look nothing like Lila." The whole notion of this was angering her deeply.

"It's all right," Mrs. Hawley said. "You see, Lila was sulking so much that I said I thought it might be good if we had her more in the shadowy part of the painting. I mean a girl with a sulky face is not especially attractive, even if she is a beauty like Lila."

"So you see, Hannah," the painter continued as his eyes traveled over Hannah from head to toe. "You are about the same height and size. And Lila was posed leaning against the vase."

"But my hair is a completely different color," Hannah protested weakly.

"No one has hair quite like yours, Hannah. It is a fascinating color, and it changes in the light." A slightly enigmatic smile played quickly across the painter's face. "But don't worry. The figure is in profile. I plan to have very dense shadows in the region of her head and face. The hair of the figure will not really be visible. But I can suggest hair. A painter must be able to inspire a viewer's imagination, evoke what might be there even if it is not." He paused and turned to Mrs. Hawley. Then he continued, "I really just need you to stand in, Hannah, so I can get the form."

"And I'm sure that Lila's dress will fit," Mrs. Hawley added.

The figure, Hannah thought. Lila had become "the figure." Mr. Wheeler was now "the painter" and Mrs. Hawley was "the client." *But what am I? The form? Oh, yes, the form! The girl in the shadows, I suppose.*

They were speaking of her as if she didn't exist, wasn't even present. How could they do this? It wasn't right. Hannah had been standing to the side during this conversation. She now placed herself squarely in front of the painter. Her eyes were bold. *Look at me!* she silently commanded. "I am not sure whether the dress will fit, sir." She then turned around and faced Mrs. Hawley. "And, ma'am, I think if Lila ever detected even a trace of me in the painting . . . it could . . ." She hesitated. "Well, it could cause much agitation."

"Oh, but, my dear, there won't be a trace of you really. Mr. Wheeler assures me of that."

Hannah turned toward the painter. "He does?" She raised one of her eyebrows. He would not look at her now.

"Oh, yes, he does. You know he is so skillful. It will be our little secret. You can keep a secret, can't you?" She did not wait for a reply but cocked her head almost flirtatiously at the painter. "And I am sure Mr. Wheeler can as well."

"I'm sure Mr. Wheeler is very good at keeping secrets," Hannah said softly, looking directly at the painter.

"It won't take long. Just a couple of sessions, really," the painter mumbled, still not looking at her.

But she found nothing assuring about the situation at all. The very thought of putting on Lila's dress was completely horrid. However, what could she do? She went into the house feeling a mixture of anger and confusion. Anger that she could be ordered to do something like this and confusion that the painter could so easily substitute her for such a loathsome person. When she was mounting the stairs to polish the wall sconces on the second floor, she caught a glimpse of the painter making his way down the driveway. She flung down her polishing cloths and raced out of the house and, taking a back way, circled through the woods so she could cut him off at the bend in the driveway. No one would see them there.

From behind the giant spruce tree where she waited, she heard his approaching footfalls on the gravel. She stepped out but not far from the tree.

"Truth! You paint the truth, sir? Is this what you call the truth, substituting me for Lila Hawley? Or perhaps you're flattering me? Is that it?"

"Hannah, no. Stop it. You know that's not how it is."

"Well, how is it? Am I supposed to feel pleased that a lowly servant, a scullery girl, is let in on a secret? I don't care about this family's secrets. Oh, yes, and I get to wear a gown instead of this uniform. It's my downstairs uniform, by the way. I'm amazed that Mrs. Hawley let me come and speak with a guest while wearing it. You know the rules, Mr. Wheeler. Not supposed to be seen in my mobcap and dusting apron. Oh, but I forgot. I'm really just a form. Lila and I are just interchangeable, so no matter — right?"

"Don't be cruel, Hannah." He walked to where she stood at the very edge of the forest on a patch of moss.

"'Cruel'? You're calling me cruel! Oh, Mr. Wheeler, that is pathetic. You are pathetic."

He dropped his eyes. "Yes, I know," he said quietly. There was something in the muted way he spoke that both touched and shocked Hannah. "I . . . I make no excuses." He suddenly stepped toward her. He wrapped his arms around her, pressing her to his chest. It was so sudden, so disorienting, that for several seconds Hannah was not precisely sure where she was — logically her mind told her she was at the edge of the drive, but she had never felt closer to the sea. She was heady with the scent of a tangy salt wind that seem to blow through her. He was kissing her lips, crushing his face against hers. She was lost. She was adrift. She was happy.

And then he was gone. He had torn himself away at the sound of an approaching carriage. He seemed to have vanished into thin air. She looked about. She stepped back into the woods just before the carriage came into view. When it was safely out of sight, she stepped back to where the painter had embraced her.

It seemed rather like a dream now. Had it really happened? It was as if she had been transported to another place, another world. The sun broke out from behind a cloud. Something glinted fiercely. She looked down. On her apron top there were two or three glistening ovals. Hannah inhaled sharply as she picked one off. And then she froze. His tears! And they were like hers, like the very ones she had shed in the music room that day.

All around her feet the moss flashed with the scintillating ovals. She stooped down and began to collect them.

It was the second day of posing. Hannah took up the position leaning against the vase while Clarice a few feet away stood facing the painter. It seemed odd now to Hannah that she had actually, for a moment back in Boston, experienced a feeling of envy when she had watched the girls posing and saw the top of

Lila's head grazing the breaking wave with the fish tail. She had felt then that Lila was claiming the sea. Lila was not of the sea nor could she ever claim it. Hannah now knew that such a thought was ridiculous.

Instead it was the vases, now so close to the sea, that she felt were in some peculiar way a portal to that world. Hannah felt great comfort wrapped in the shadow the vase cast on this morning. Yet at the same time it suddenly struck her that the painter was a portal as well. She slid her eyes toward him. He was mixing some more paints. She touched the pouch. She had his tears, inexplicably transformed, mingled with her own in the pouch.

Something had happened when they had kissed. All her feelings of resentment had vanished. She knew she was not a substitute. No one would ever be able to tell that the figure, the form, was not Lila. But it was Hannah he was painting. His eyes moved over her slowly, lingering. She could hear the whispered strokes of the brush; they were palpable, almost as she had felt his kisses. And that was the real secret.

He would make excuses to come over and adjust the collar or the hem of her dress. Always of course careful to attend to something with Clarice's or Ettie's dress as well. He would suddenly be standing in front of Hannah, touching the ruffled edge of the collar. "I just need to adjust it," he spoke softly in an almost apologetic voice. They could even joke about the gown now. "Not that different from the dress you wear for your chores, is it?"

"Very different, sir. It is all very different," Hannah whispered. He let his finger graze the side of her neck. She flinched, shut her eyes, but treasured the fleeting moment.

The posing was extended for more than a week. He attributed this to the fog that rolled in and out, saying that it took longer for certain areas to dry and therefore he had to work slower. Ettie suggested that she could fan the painting every morning and evening to accelerate drying. She had a lovely fan from her grandmother. But the painter was adamant. It must dry naturally.

Eight days later the painting was finished. The Hawleys planned to have a party to show it to their friends. There was already talk that this was one of the best Stannish Whitman Wheeler paintings ever and that it would most likely be transported next winter across the Atlantic to be displayed at the famous Salon de Paris, the greatest event of the art world. The party to unveil the painting would be a very grand one. A ball with an orchestra was coming from Boston. A concert pianist and harpist would also perform. A pastry chef would be imported from New York. No expense would be spared. And Ettie would be allowed to attend her first grown-up party in a special dress that was being sewn by the best seamstress in the village. Upon hearing this, Ettie had replied, "I'd rather wear my bathing costume. I hate fancy dresses in the summertime."

"SOME NEWS"

IT WAS ONLY A WEEK later that Mr. Marston walked into the kitchen just as the servants were settling down for their noonday meal. He had a curious, almost bewildered look on his face. They all immediately sensed that he was about to make an announcement, but not with his usual assertive bearing and commanding attitude. His eyes darted nervously about the kitchen. He cleared his throat, coughed, and then began.

"Well, we've had some . . . some . . ." He hesitated. "We've had some news," he said with a slight break in his voice. He looked down and seemed to study his shoes for a few seconds and then, regaining his composure, he looked up and smiled brightly. His eyes remained grim. "Jade has been found safe and sound. This was a few days ago actually, although I was just informed." They could all tell Mr. Marston was decidedly miffed that he had not been informed earlier.

"Now where the devil did they find the cursed cat?" Mrs. Bletchley asked.

"Oh, she wandered back, reeking of fish. No doubt she went for a holiday on T Wharf. Chauncey said she stunk to high heaven. She even had some scales in the fur of her paws."

"Too bad she didn't get a bone stuck in her gullet," Mrs. Bletchley snorted.

"Now, now, Mrs. Bletchley. At least here Jade won't have to go so far afield for her holiday repasts. Plenty of fish nearby." Hannah felt a shiver go through her entire body.

"She should have drowned!" Daze muttered.

Mr. Marston took a deep breath. "And seeing as Lila has been making a steady recovery, both she and Jade will be returning." They all tried their best not to groan, but a massive silent sigh seemed to suspend itself in the air of the kitchen.

"When, might I ask?" Mrs. Bletchley said, looking up from one of her interminable lists.

"The eleven o'clock steamer this Thursday," Mr. Marston replied tersely. "Now, if you will excuse me, I have much to attend to and shall have to take something to eat later, Mrs. Bletchley. I hope this does not inconvenience you."

"Oh, no," said Mrs. Bletchley softly. They were all thinking the same thing at that moment. The inconvenience was not Mr. Marston's skipping lunch, but Lila Hawley and the damn cat's coming to the beautiful island.

The portrait party was how they were all referring to the grand ball at which the painting of the Hawley daughters would be unveiled. If one went into the village, to the post office or Bee's or down on the pier, all one heard talk of was the Hawleys' party, or "party for a painting," as the locals were inclined to call it. It seemed to affect the entire village and its citizenry — natives, rusticators, mealers, hauled mealers, and cottagers. It was the most coveted invitation of the summer.

Extra help had been hired for the affair. And sleeping accommodations had been found for the orchestra and the pastry chef from New York, in addition to Mrs. Wickmore Bellamy, Boston's foremost floral designer. It was a difficult time of year, for August was the busiest month on the island and most of the hotels were full up, as well as the rent houses. But when one had money, as Perl said, one could have anything one wanted — a-yuh. Mr. Hawley had rented an entire house for the musicians and other people who were to be brought in for the party.

There were, of course, whispers about Lila Hawley — a fragile beauty — but then again there was that immense wealth. An undeniable catch. The party was perceived as the lead-up to her debut. Debuts were where the real auction for American heiresses began. Of late these coming-out parties, as they were called, had been frequented by titled young gentlemen from England who came to peruse the goods. How else could those depleted aristocratic fortunes be shored up without the new money of this new American aristocracy that had built railroads — or sold the plows to dig the tracks for railroads or the steel to lay the tracks, or tapped into the vast underground riches of coal and oil to fuel the growing energy needs of a country on the move in every sense of the word?

"How does she look?" Susie said as Florrie and Daze came into the kitchen during dinner two nights later. No one had seen Lila since she had arrived that morning.

"About the same, I think," Florrie said. "What do you think, Daze?"

"About the same, I'd say," Daze replied.

"Well, I hope at least rested. They call it a rest cure, for pity's sake," Mrs. Bletchley said as she furiously beat some egg whites and then scowled into the bowl. "You know, trying to get egg whites to set up on an island surrounded by water, and not to mention fog for the last two days, is really impossible. Maybe that fancy New York pastry chef can do it. Imagine sending all the way to New York for a pastry chef! It's a wonder they didn't ship that fellow in from Paris," she muttered. Mrs. Bletchley's nose had been out of joint since it was first announced that the pastry chef was coming.

"Well, did she look rested?" Hannah asked.

"Yes, I suppose so," Daze said reflectively. "But her eyes looked sort of funny."

"Funny?" Willy asked. He had just come in from getting the yacht, *Desperate Lark*, ready for the next day's sailing picnic. "You mean like ha-ha funny?"

"No, I mean like queer funny. Droopy."

"It's all that stuff they give them nervous ladies," Mrs. Bletchley said.

Mr. Marston came in at that moment to fetch two more bottles of wine. "I don't think we are in a position to be discussing medical treatment, Mrs. Bletchley."

"Laudanum!" Mrs. Bletchley said and held up the whisk she was using to beat the egg whites. "That's the word I was looking for. My sister-in-law took it. Drugged her, it did."

"She probably did not take it in consultation with a doctor, Mrs. Bletchley," Mr. Marston said. There was a decided edge to his voice. Daze, Florrie, Susie, and Hannah exchanged looks. They knew that Mr. Marston and Mrs. Bletchley secretly enjoyed their little arguments and this looked like the start of one.

"What does a consultation have to do with it, I ask?" Mrs. Bletchley countered and looked fiercely at the butler.

"Laudanum is an analgesic. Administered properly, it alleviates anxiety and induces sleep." Mr. Marston tried to cow Mrs. Bletchley by using as many big words as he could. But the cook remained undaunted. Looking as if she were about to beat the living daylights out of the egg whites, she lowered her voice and appeared to address the bowl's recalcitrant contents.

"Drugs, pure and simple. They might as well have sent her to an opium den."

"Really, Mrs. Bletchley!" Mr. Marston took the wine bottles and walked out of the kitchen in a huff.

Willy looked up from the thumbnail he was picking at. "Game, set, match, Mrs. Bletchley. You won that one."

Mrs. Bletchley shook her head. "Tennis, fresh air,

exercise. The girl don't need no laudanum. She needs good food and why not blueberry pie? Why in the name of heaven can't we be having blueberry pie, for pity's sake, instead of this ridiculous meringue dessert? It's blueberry season in Maine. Finest blueberries in the entire world. Little Ettie has been aching for blueberry pie. Bless her heart, sometimes I think she's the only sane one in the family. You know she goes right out to that field beyond the orchard and eats them off the bush whenever she can escape Miss Ardmore."

"Don't I know it," Hannah said. "Her clothes are all stained blue. I can't tell you how much time I spend rubbing Javelle water into those stains."

"And you're using the Fels-Naptha soap with it, aren't you?" Florrie asked.

"A-yuh," Hannah replied, then they all laughed.

"Getting to sound like a real downeaster, you are," Daze said.

"Indeed," Hannah said almost wistfully. She wished they could stay here forever. Why did Lila have to come? She'd only been there a short time, but already tension was felt in the house.

A LARGE DARK EYE

Hᴀɴɴᴀʜ ᴡᴀѕ ѕɪᴛᴛɪɴɢ on the bow of the sleek sailing yacht with her legs dangling over the side, next to Willy. She had been overjoyed when Ettie had specially requested that she come.

The reason was classic Ettie. "You must let Hannah come, Daddy, because you know how bored I can get with all those grown-ups chattering away. And when I get bored, I get whiny. And sometimes even cranky! But I never do when Hannah is around. So I can talk to her at the first second of boring-ness."

"Hannah, you're a fearless girl. Hang on!" Willy shouted as the yacht tipped.

"I love it when it does this. What do you call it, Willy?"

"Heeling. But Captain Eaton is not flying much sail in this wind because the ladies always squeal when it heels too much." The movement of the yacht slicing through the water was one of the most incredible sensations Hannah had ever known. She looked down at the bow splitting the water, flinging up wings of spray. She felt the thrum of the rigging as the wind punched into the sails. There were water rustlings, the crush of the sea foam against the hull of the boat, the rhythm of the waves and the pull of the wind, all weaving together into a beautiful song of the sea that she could listen to forever. *Forever*, she thought.

Just then a little piercing voice carried over the wind, "I'm borrrred! Hannah, come get me!"

"Better go get Ettie," Hannah said.

"I'll go. And I'll get a line to tether her, even though she's wearing a life preserver. Mr. Hawley doesn't like her out of the cockpit without a line on her."

Ettie was smiling as she walked unevenly with Willy behind her on the rocking deck. "Things got boring back there, did they?" Hannah laughed.

"Oh, brother!" Ettie sighed and plopped down next to Hannah.

"Let me tie you in, Ettie," Willy said.

"Dumb!" Ettie replied. But she looked very happy to be on the foredeck with Hannah and Willy.

Suddenly Hannah felt an almost magical energy surrounding the yacht. Her feet and legs began to tingle and then she felt a quiver in the pouch beneath her dress. A spirit seemed to be rising up within her to meet the energy coming from the water. She touched the pouch lightly.

Am I finally ready? she wondered. *Is this it?* A deep strain, not unlike the vibrations from the harp that came to her that stormy night, began to emanate from the water. *Something is there . . . calling to me. . . .* She listened carefully. Through the hum of the wind in the sails and the soft crushing sound of the waves against the hull, Hannah began to hear a sequence of clicks and squeaks. There were even whistles. But she was not sure if she was hearing these sounds with her ears or if she was feeling them. She stole a glance at Willy and Ettie. *Are they hearing this, too?* she wondered. But she could tell they weren't.

I know you are here! Was it a thought? Was it actual words she had spoken? No. Not out loud, but somehow she had expressed a message and was being answered.

At just that moment the cry "Dolphins!" cut across the wind.

"Oh, great!" Willy said, jumping up. Just beneath the surface Hannah spotted the sleek gray shapes.

"Look at them, Hannah, Ettie!" Willy said. "They love the waves off the bow when we're going this fast. Watch them coast."

"There are millions of them," Ettie said. Then she called down to the dolphins. "Stay here, dolphins, at the bow. It is so boring back there!"

The water seemed almost braided with the sleek forms of the dolphins. When they rolled onto their sides the lighter skin of their flanks flashed through the dark green water like pale licks of flame. They seemed to be showing off. Sometimes they swam in couples and they would dip and arc over each other and never so much as touch.

"It's like they're trying to show off just for us, isn't it?" Hannah sighed happily as she watched them.

"You know," said Ettie thoughtfully. "You have to be kind of smart to show off. It's almost like they are not just animals." She paused. "Look, Hannah!" she shrieked. "That one's come up and is looking right at you."

Hannah looked down. Her eyes widened. The dolphin was looking directly at her. The large dark eye framed by folds of skin seemed to peer right into her own eyes. Something clicked in her brain. *This creature knows me . . . knows me in ways others do not. It knows me. But how?*

"Look, Hannah! That dolphin is saying hello just to you," Ettie cried with delight.

"Don't lean over too far, Hannah," Willy said. But Hannah ignored him.

Wait! Your time will come. The words were not spoken aloud, but they flowed up to her, right through her legs and feet, which dangled over the edge.

"Don't fall in, Hannah!" Ettie shrieked. "I would die if you drowned." There was real terror in Ettie's voice. But Hannah didn't hear it. She felt she was almost through that portal, the one she had sensed, smelled in the shadowy interior of the vase. She knew she was halfway there, halfway to a new world.

Wait! commanded the mysterious voice that was not a voice at all.

⚜   ⚜   ⚜

"Wasn't that a lovely sail, darling?" Mrs. Hawley was saying to Lila later that afternoon as Hannah brought the tea tray to the porch and set it down.

"Yes," Lila replied numbly. The cat sat on her lap snoozing.

"And the portrait ball is going to be so marvelous. Why, Ettie will be attending her first grown-up party."

Lila turned her head very slowly. "Aren't you excited, Ettie?" she asked almost mechanically.

"No, because what I really wanted was to have my birthday party on that very day. August fifteenth."

"But it's not . . ." Lila seemed to have intended to comment more on Ettie's birthday, but she sank back against the pillows of the wicker couch as if she was too exhausted to say another word.

During the few days they had been at Gladrock, both Jade and her mistress had seemed to be in a vague state, halfway between waking and sleeping. No one was sure if Lila did actually sleep. Ettie told Hannah that Lila's eyes never closed completely. Ettie had sneaked into her room when supposedly she was taking an afternoon nap.

"She was breathing just like she was asleep, you know." Ettie imitated the slow rhythmic breathing of sleep with the muffled sounds of a soft snore at its edges. "Her eyes were half open, but when I called her name, she never even stirred."

"What about the cat?" Hannah had asked.

"Never blinked an eye. She seemed asleep, too. But her eyes were just half closed." It occurred to Hannah that perhaps the Hawleys were giving the cat the laudanum as well. On two separate occasions Lila had been found sleepwalking upstairs with her eyes fully open but not in a conscious state. Instructions had been issued that if anyone encountered Lila this way, they were not to try to wake her for the effect could be too startling. Instead they were to take her gently by the hand and lead her back to bed, and then come and inform the Hawleys.

A few seconds after Ettie had begun to tell her about the birthday party, Lila roused herself and asked, "When do we get to see the portrait, Mummy?"

"Oh, not now, darling. We want it to be a surprise."

"Have Ettie and Clarice seen it?"

"Nope," Ettie answered.

"Don't say nope, dear." Mrs. Hawley turned to Ettie. "It's so common."

Ettie got a wicked twinkle in her eye. "A-yuh!" she said and ran out of the room.

❧   ❧   ❧

"Ah! Ettie." Mrs. Weed came bustling in. Mrs. Weed was the head housekeeper at Gladrock, for

Miss Horton always went back to Canada to visit her relatives in the summer. "Miss Beale just arrived to fit your dress for the party."

"I don't want to be fitted for a stupid party dress. I don't want to wear a dress. I want to wear my bathing costume."

"But I've never seen such a pretty color dress, de-ah," Mrs. Weed said. "Just the color of blueberries."

"That was on purpose. See, it won't be any problem if I get it stained, because I *looove* blueberries."

Mrs. Weed laughed. "Well, are you planning on going blueberry picking during the party?"

"I wish! It's the best time for blueberries. Best time for shooting stars, too, and Uncle Barkley gave me a telescope. Best time for everything except a fancy-dancy party." One minute her voice had bubbled up in irrepressible enthusiasm, but suddenly Ettie's shoulders sank, her head drooped to one side, and she half closed her eyes in deep reflection, and then, with a wistfulness that seemed beyond her years, she said, "I can't think of anything lovelier than lying down in a field of blueberries on a hot August night or floating in the cove and looking up at the sky and waiting for stars to fall. A party, or at least that kind of a party, is the last place I want to be." She shook her head almost mournfully. She wasn't angry or stubborn anymore, she just seemed resigned.

GET OUT, HANNAH! GET OUT!

IT WAS THE EVENING of the party, and outside, thick fog swirled across the lawn. A dozen maids in dark green uniforms with crisply starched, lace-trimmed aprons passed hors d'oeuvres. "Well, at least it's cloudy," Hannah whispered to Ettie. "So you're not missing any falling stars."

"What are these?" Ettie said, looking down at the canapés.

"Crabmeat on a biscuit. Very good."

Ettie took one and Hannah moved on, winding through the crowd of people. There were at least one hundred guests. Many had come for this special evening from as far away as Boston and Newport, Rhode Island. The Hawleys were known for their lavish parties, lavish at least by Boston standards, and Mrs. Hawley in particular was known for her sense of style. The combination of the Hawleys and the world-famous painter Stannish Whitman Wheeler was unbeatable. Hannah could even detect the glint of envy in some of the women's eyes. As she moved through the guests with her platter, she picked up scraps of conversation.

"They say it is an extraordinary painting . . . a departure for him."

"Who can say anything? Who's seen it?"

Hannah saw a very elegant lady flip open her fan and use it to shield her mouth while she spoke, but her eyes followed Lila. Despite the Hawleys' extra-ordinary attempts to conceal their daughter's condition and her whereabouts for most of the sum-mer, there was still talk. Daze and Susie had heard it in the village. And several people in the room now were stealing glances at Lila.

Lila looked exquisite in a flowing, pale pink chiffon gown with a cluster of silk flowers at her waist. She also appeared more alert than she had been since her arrival at Gladrock. But Hannah was nervous. Was there any chance that Lila would see something in the painter's depiction that would give the merest hint that Hannah had stood in her place? Hannah prayed that somehow she would not be in the room for the unveiling.

She heard the tinkle of a little bell. *Good heavens!* This was happening much faster than Hannah had anticipated. She was in the middle of the room with a platter almost full of canapés. The rules were that servants could not return to the kitchen to replenish a tray until more than three-quarters of it had been consumed. She had half a mind to stuff the rest into her mouth. A hush was settling on the crowd. With Willy's help, Mr. Marston was rolling out a large stand against which the painting rested, draped in cloth. Horace Hawley now stepped forward with Stannish Whitman Wheeler at his side.

"Ladies and gentlemen, welcome to Gladrock on this very special evening." He then turned to his daughters. "It is a special evening for Edwina and myself because we have been blessed with three especially lovely daughters. And although the essence of life is change, growing older and hopefully wiser, there is no one amongst us who has not wished to arrest time. Well, it cannot be done. We cannot slip the mortal chains for a tryst with immortality. But a consummate artist, a genius, can help us imagine such things. There is nothing Edwina and I want more than a long and healthy life for each of our daughters, and yet we also yearn to capture them in the moments that have been precious to us. Tonight they stand before you as elegant young ladies — or almost young ladies." He was looking at Ettie, who was turning bright red with embarrassment. It was at that moment that Hannah noticed that Ettie was wearing her black rubberized bathing shoes under her long gown. *My Lord in heaven, what is she planning?* Should she tell Florrie, Daze, Perl? But her thought broke off as she saw Mr. Marston and Willy begin to loosen the drape. Mrs. Hawley now stepped forward and pulled a braided cord. The cloth fell.

There was absolute silence as people took in the painting. Ettie, like a luminous spirit, was in the foreground, behind her Clarice stood solemnly, her honest face trusting and open. But the background of the painting was dense with shadows, and against the vase was the dark figure of Lila, her shoulders flung back, pressing against its blue and white design.

"Very modern," Hannah heard someone whisper.

"Wheeler is master of chiaroscuro."

"But it's so dark . . . I mean how would one even know that is Lila lurking back there?"

"But it's riveting, you have to admit." It was the voice of a young man. "This is what art should be about. Not the obvious, not simple biography. It is as if these children have been caught in the midst of play, a game interrupted, but a game we'll never understand." He paused. "At least we outsiders."

"Yes, I quite agree," another gentleman said. "Despite Wheeler's youth it seems as if he has a rather old soul. An understanding beyond his years. There is no one like Wheeler for suggesting the unknowable."

Hannah inhaled sharply upon hearing this remark. Could these gentlemen ever know how true their words were? There was certainly some sort of secret at the very center of the painter's being. Perhaps it was this secret that made him a great painter, but he guarded it as if it were gold. Soon the room was buzzing with conversation. Hannah glanced across the room toward the painter. He stood near the portrait, surrounded by guests. Women in particular pressed to get close to him. She was suddenly filled with a deep and urgent yearning. She drifted closer with her tray of hors d'oeuvres.

"He says he never makes appointments at receptions or parties," said one young lady.

"I understand he's booked for the next two years," a gentleman added. While they talked, their eyes were on the painting, pressing closer to it — everyone's eyes except for two people in the room. As Hannah turned her head, she saw Lila's eyes staring straight at her. The vague look had vanished and two glittering blue-green gemstone eyes flickered with an undeniable and profound hatred.

At just that moment, Hannah felt something swish under her skirt. "Ooow!" Her platter fell to the floor. There was a white streak across the room.

"A cat!" someone shrieked.

Hannah was mortified. Surely she would be fired. She dropped to her knees and began gathering up the canapés. Tears were streaming down her face. Mr. Marston was beside her in a minute.

"Don't worry, dear, not your fault," he said kindly, but his hands were trembling. "I don't know how that cat got in here." He stood up and someone else was bending over her.

"Get out, Hannah, my dear. Get out. You're ready! Your time has almost come!" a voice whispered in her ear. Hannah looked into the painter's green eyes. In them she saw worlds she had suspected but never known and the dim shadow of regret for a wildness lost.

"Ready?" she whispered.

"Yes, you are ready."

"But . . . but I must leave you," Hannah said. There was a choking desperation in her voice.

"Forget about me."

"But you are my —" But the painter was already walking away. His words reverberated through her.

She clutched at the pouch. Ready? Her time had come?

⚜ ⚜ ⚜

"You're bleeding!" Susie said a few minutes later, in the kitchen.

Bleeding? What do I care about a little blood? Hannah thought.

"I'm going to kill that cat!" Mrs. Bletchley hissed. "You stay right here in the kitchen with me, dearie. They don't need you out there. Susie, get the iodine. I'll bring over some soapy water."

Hannah was sitting on a stool and rolling down her bloody stocking. There was a long scratch that ran up her calf. "It's not that bad, Mrs. Bletchley. Look, it's stopped bleeding already."

"Yes, but you don't want to get an infection. Now you just sit right there. I'm going to get you a cup of tea."

Mr. Marston came in. "Is everything all right, Hannah? Mr. and Mrs. Hawley are appalled."

Appalled? Hannah looked at him expectantly. Would

he call her into his office at Gladrock and quietly say she must go, but give her perhaps a week before she had to leave and a dollar or so? Or would he fire her outright in front of everyone?

"I'm really sorry, Mr. Marston. I should have seen the cat."

"Nonsense, child! You've nothing to apologize for. They are appalled at the cat."

"What about Lila — shouldn't she be appalled?" Mrs. Bletchley asked.

"Actually, she was very sorry and sends her apologies," Mr. Marston said.

"Well, that's a change." Mrs. Bletchley pulled down her mouth and raised her eyebrows with a look of astonishment.

"In any case, the cat has been locked in Lila's room. She even agreed. In that sense I really do see some improvement in her. She was quite docile and took her directly upstairs."

Docile, my foot! Hannah thought to herself. She didn't trust Lila, nor did she trust all the talk she had heard upon Lila's return of her "improvement." It was nothing but a play, a feint. An opening move in combat. Lila was set to destroy her. *And if it is a fight she wants — well, she'll have it!* But of course Hannah would betray none of this. She would appear as "docile" as her opponent.

"I just don't want a fuss made," Hannah said meekly. "Really, please, no fuss. I'm going to get a clean stocking and I'd like to help again. I don't want to make too much of it."

Mr. Marston smiled at her warmly. "You're quite a trouper, Hannah, quite a trouper!"

After she had changed her stockings, Hannah went back into the dining room. "You sure you want to serve that side of the table?" Florrie said. "You'll have to serve Lila."

"Exactly!"

But Lila never looked up when Hannah came to her first with the sauce for the swordfish, then with the salad plate, and finally with the dessert, profiteroles on a pond of chocolate sauce. "Care for some more, Miss Lila?" Hannah came around with the sauce boat of chocolate even though she could see that

Lila needed none. Lila did not look up but merely shook her head. Hannah felt the painter's eyes following her as she continued around the table.

"Hi, Hannah. You all right?" Ettie said, looking up as she came by with the chocolate sauce.

"Hello, Ettie. I don't think you're supposed to talk with me, dear. Not at a fancy party like this."

"I don't care. I'll talk with whomever I please."

Hannah knew she should not encourage any conversation. So she moved on.

After the dinner was finished, the guests went to the second floor of the house where there was a grand ballroom. The orchestra had been tuning up. Hannah had been excused early by Mr. Marston and for this she was glad. She had made her point with Lila and did not need to see her dancing with all the young men of Bar Harbor.

Shortly before midnight the party finally ended. Daze, Susie, and Florrie all had beaux in the village and had planned to go out after the party and meet them. There was quite a bit of courting in the summertime — courtships between servants of one cottage and another and between servants and natives as well. They often went over to Eagle Lake and had bonfires on the beach or took canoes out for midnight paddles. Hannah had only gone once and did not particularly enjoy it. She found lake water sterile compared with the sea's. And tonight, exhausted as she was, Hannah was only too happy to undress and crawl into bed. She looked out of the round window. A heavy fog had rolled in. *Might as well be looking into a full milk bottle*, she thought. She turned down the wick of her oil lamp. The second her head hit the pillow, she fell into a dreamless sleep.

THE TAIL IN THE WAVE

SHE WASN'T SURE WHAT it was that awakened her. She had no idea what time it was. Then she saw the figure standing at the foot of her bed, as still as a statue. Her eyes open, but glazed. The cat in her arms, perfectly still. Like pieces of a puzzle coming together, the bizarre reality began to assemble itself. Lila had sleepwalked up here. The cat was almost limp in her arms, and appeared to be in some sort of hypnotic state, its eyes half shut and glazed. Hannah remembered the instructions. She must take Lila by the hand and lead her back to her room. Then she must go and wake the Hawleys.

Ever so slowly, Hannah slipped out of bed. She quickly grabbed for her nightgown on the bedpost.

Then she walked up to Lila. Without saying a word she took her hand and began to lead her from the room. They descended the first set of the back stairs, and then the next to the family bedrooms. She was about to lead Lila through the back stairway door to the corridor when Lila wrenched her hand away.

Lila's eyes were wild. She was scratching at Hannah's face and the cat suddenly came to life and pounced on her back. Hannah could feel the claws digging into her shoulders, close to the neck of the nightgown. She looked down and saw the two huge paws clasped onto her collarbones and scratching at the string from which the pouch hung.

Hannah fell to the floor but quickly staggered to her feet. She was gasping for breath and with horror realized that the cat had shifted and was no longer on her back, but hanging by the pouch strings from her neck. She looked down. There was something so freakish about the cat's paws. Then she realized it was the six toes Roseanne had told her about. Jade was using them as deftly as fingers, pulling the string of the pouch and those that closed the neckline of the nightgown tighter and tighter. Lila stood aside, her eyes feverish. Her youth had vanished, replaced by a fury of purpose. Her face was a contorted mask of absolute determination and every trace of humanity was gone. At first it sounded like a purr coming from Lila's throat but then she heard the words — "Freckles, does she have freckles?"

The strings of Hannah's pouch were cutting into her throat, and she was gasping for air. A rent had been torn in the pouch and a radiant mist flowed from it, as if an artery to her heart had been sliced open. Only it was not blood, it was her soul. *No! No!* The word screeched in her head.

The world was turning black. She could not let this happen! She would not! Hannah felt anger growing in her, and then the power she sensed within herself surged, building like an immense wave. She hurled herself forward, slamming into a wall. There was a terrible screech from the cat, then a crash as they tumbled down the stairs together.

"Stop! Stop!" Ettie was at the top of the stairs, but Hannah was no longer listening. She had to get away. She tore out of the door that led into the kitchen and then onto the back porch. Lila ran after her. Hannah looked over her shoulder. She could outrun her, but it was hard to see Jade in the thick fog. "Go back, Ettie!" Hannah called. "Get help!"

Hannah had not thought where to run. The fog had enveloped everything in an impenetrable, gauzy whiteness. A thick quiet had descended. It seemed more day than night and no land features were discernible in the shifting miasma of vapors, stirring as soundlessly as ghosts. But suddenly Hannah could hear everything from the slight rustle of a blown leaf to the movement of a blade of grass or the quiver of sea lavender as water from the incoming tide licked its stems. She trembled and touched her chest. The pouch was gone, and yet she thought, *I am here! My time has come!*

Hannah reached the lavender rock, washed by a high tide. The bottom of her nightgown was drenched, and she could hear the click of the cat's claws on the rocks just behind her. She stretched her arms forward and arced into the air as a distinct sound came to her — the shattering of porcelain.

The next thing she knew, Hannah was beneath the surface of the water. It was deep. Her feet did not touch the bottom. But that did not matter.

She felt the swirl of the water around her. It was not cold, and it cushioned and caressed her. She stretched out and began to swim across the cove, sometimes diving deeply and swimming beneath the surface. She could hold her breath for long minutes. Despite the dark, she saw around her a shifting land-scape of swaying tawny sea grapes on amber fronds, and all sorts of rocks. She circled Perl's dory, which was tethered to a mooring block. Her eyes picked out the antennae of a lobster protruding from the slot in a rock.

The longer she swam, the more Hannah knew that she had not merely jumped into a cove, she had become part of a floating world of music. The water had its tones. Some were dark and amber, some pure gold.

And just as there was a spectrum of color and hues that amazed her eyes, there was a range of rhythms caused by currents and eddies. She quickly learned how to swim through these currents, adjusting the power of her strokes to the pressure of the water that flowed around her. She was astonished by the bursts of speed she could achieve. It was not simply her arms that were carrying her through the water — there was an incredible power coming from her legs and yet her legs no longer felt the same.

She swam toward the surface and rolled onto her back. A sudden wind had sprung up and scraped off the fog, and she could see that the black sky was powdered with stars. She lifted her legs from the water, blinked. There was a scintillation in the moonlight. She blinked, then blinked again. Glistening teardrop shapes spangled the darkness. "Those aren't legs," Hannah whispered. "It's a tail. A tail like the one breaking out of the wave painted on the vase."

Impossible! But no, not at all! Her season had

come. The world that was hinted at in the painting on the vase had been realized. She had in fact passed through the portal, had crossed over, and had found not a diabolical spirit, not a tormenting wraith, and not a demon familiar, but a part of her natural history, her heritage, her family. And even if she was right now the only member of that family, she felt whole at last, complete.

Oh, they were all right, she wanted to shout. *I am perfectly unsuitable! I am not an orphan, I am a daughter of the sea!* Hannah knew that she was home at last. A sound scratched the night, a child crying somewhere. It tugged on her, but it seemed so far away that it was easy not to heed it, and she felt a wonderful current pulling on her. She dived back beneath the surface. The sound stopped. Hannah swam deeper to find the pulse of the current.

❧ ❧ ❧

A small figure raced across the lawn and through the meadow at the edge of the sea, crying, "She's drowned! She's drowned! She's gone! Gone forever!"

People were now running from the house in their nightclothes.

Mr. Marston, barefoot, his dressing gown flying out behind him, arrived, followed by Mr. Hawley and several servants.

"What's happened, child?" Mr. Marston asked.

"What in God's name is going on?" another voice cried.

"Hannah! Hannah!" Ettie sobbed, and between the sobs she was hiccuping.

"What happened to Hannah?" Mr. Hawley asked. "Lila, why are you scratched? You're bleeding."

"She chased her!" Ettie finally roared. "Lila chased Hannah into the sea. Lila and Jade." Lila stood there, unmoving.

"Lila?" Mr. Hawley said, walking slowly toward his daughter. "Lila, my dear, is this true?"

"Hannah killed Jade," Lila said, and pointed to a clump of blood-soaked sea lavender where Jade was sprawled. The cat's head was twisted at an odd angle to its body. One side was bashed in and there was a mangled mash of fur and protruding bone.

"That's a lie," Ettie screamed. "Hannah did no such thing." Ettie looked at her older sister. "I killed Jade!"

Lila exploded and hurled herself across the grass, knocking down her sister. Her hand was reaching for a rock when Mr. Marston ran up and dragged her off Ettie.

"Take her away," Mr. Hawley said. He was shaking as he gathered Ettie into his arms.

"Horace! Horace! What is going on here?" Edwina Hawley had just arrived and was looking frantically from her husband to her eldest daughter, who was held by Mr. Marston and Willy. But Lila was not struggling. She looked at Ettie, whose lip was bleeding, and calmly said, "When you killed Jade, you killed me. I am dead because of you."

"I want Hannah! I want Hannah!" It was all Ettie could say through her bleeding lips.

"Don't worry, dear," Mr. Hawley said. But his words hardly belied his agitation. His eyes were fixed on Ettie's bloody mouth. He tore off the cuff of his nightshirt and began trying to staunch the flow of blood. His face had turned pale beneath his summer tan, and he turned to Perl. "Perl, get Captain Eaton and some of the others and go out in the motor launch and search for Hannah. We'll find her, dear." Then he shouted, "Get me a damn cloth, this child is bleeding!"

"She said she could swim," Ettie whimpered.

THIS NEW WORLD

HANNAH SWAM INTO the dawn. She had no idea when she surfaced near Egg Rock Lighthouse that there were at least half a dozen boats and motor launches out scouring the coast, from the cove to Great Head and then on from Great Head south all the way to Otter Creek. The tide had turned and it was ebbing. It would be logical that Hannah or anyone who had fallen into the sea would be carried south. The tidal currents would be too strong to swim against — if one were a mere human. But Hannah knew with certainty as she circled Egg Rock that she was not.

I am not human. I am a mermaid. And she laughed when she thought how mermaids supposedly were make-believe creatures from fairy tales. *But I am real!*

she exclaimed to herself. Suddenly a thought struck her so hard she had to stop swimming. She broke through the surface, and rolling onto her back, she looked up into the lilac morning sky. *And if I am a mermaid, is the painter a merman? I must tell him what has happened. I must show him. Show him this!*

She lifted her tail from the sea and began to examine it closely. It was beautiful. Delicate scales ranged in hue from gold to green to sapphire. The colors paled as they reached the flukes of her tail, which were silvery with a rose tinge. She could hardly remember what it felt like to have toes and feet, and when she tried to recall the feeling of wiggling her toes, the flukes of her tail stirred slightly. Yet she knew that this tail was powerful. It could drive her from the water into high arcing dives above the surface.

Was she to live here forever? She loved it. But where in the vastness of the sea would she live? The word *forever* tugged at the back of her mind, and a slightly ominous feeling shimmered through her. There was something that she could not exactly recall. Like a persistent current it drew her back to land, a current she could not quite swim against. Then she remembered — the painter — that shadow of regret she had seen in his eyes. In that instant she knew that the painter who had come from the sea could not go back — ever.

Would she really give up all she had right now, all this happiness, this beauty that she had felt in the last few hours, all this music that had streamed through her? But she knew that she would have to return, if only one more time. She must see the painter again.

But could she? Could she become a creature of land again? And did it have to be for always? Could she somehow manage to live in both worlds? Would she be able to recover her legs just to walk? She must try to get back to land, to Gladrock, if only to say good-bye to the painter and to see if Ettie was all right. That scream she had heard began to scratch at her heart.

It did not take her long to swim back. The shore was very steep just south of the cove of Gladrock, where cliffs poured like liquid granite into the sea. It was a dangerous place to swim or even boat. Caves slashed the cliffs where the water had furrowed in. Hannah thought that perhaps she could hide in the shadows of this cliff and see if she could return to her human form.

She swam into a cave as far back as she could to where she saw some dry rock, then clambered out of the water and heaved her tail high onto the rock ledge. Miraculously her nightgown was still intact. If she did resume her human form, she could hardly walk up to Gladrock naked. She peered again at the tail and tried very hard to remember her feet, her toes, her knees, and all the parts of her limbs that seemed to have melted into this gloriously beautiful and powerful tail. She grabbed a wad of seaweed and began patting the tail to dry it off. A slight stinging sensation began to tingle near her flukes. She rubbed her tail hard now with her hands. Was that a knee she felt? She pressed her fingers over the rounded lump. She rubbed it harder. The scales were growing duller. She felt a stirring at the very tip and then a pulling apart in the two lobes of the fluked tail. "My feet!" she whispered. The transformation took less than two minutes. She bent her legs and felt slightly dismayed. The feeling was not of having regained something, but quite the opposite — having lost something she had just found.

She wiggled her toes, then slowly stood up, shook out each leg, and bent it several times. *And now, I suppose I must walk out of here.* Just before she tried to stand up, her hand automatically went to where the pouch had hung for so many months. There was no cool radiance, only the dim memory. She closed her eyes and whispered, "It was only a symbol. A sign. I know what I am now." She hesitated. "Or what I can be."

⚜ ⚜ ⚜

There was a ledge of rock along the side of the cave and it was dry. If she inched along it, she could reach a place she had spotted at the mouth of the cave where she could begin to climb up the cliff. It would give the easiest approach to dry land.

On land it all seemed so different. In the water of the bay she felt wrapped in a sensory splendor of heightened color and light and movement. She felt a part of all of it. But here there was no song wrapping around her, no stirrings within her. She felt a discontinuity between herself and this world, and recognized how completely separate and isolated all things were out of the water. She suddenly felt very vulnerable. It was all she could do to take a step forward. But she had arrived at the edge of Gladrock's orchard. Hidden by the apple trees, she could see people standing in the driveway where a closed carriage had pulled up, which was unusual for the island. Most families drove about in buckboards or dainty hansoms with awnings that could be extended when it rained. This, however, was a city carriage. She could see two figures dressed in some sort of uniforms — nurses, it suddenly dawned on her. They were leading another figure down the steps of Gladrock to the carriage. It was Lila! And standing in the drive were Mr. and Mrs. Hawley and, yes, Ettie! She stood next to her sister Clarice! *Ettie is all right! I don't belong here. As long as Ettie is all right . . . but the painter? Where is the painter?* She closed her eyes and remembered his thrilling face.

Just at that moment Ettie turned her head slightly.

"Hannah!" Ettie's voice split the air. "She's back, Mummy! She's back!" Ettie broke away and began running across the field just as the carriage pulled out of the drive.

"Hannah, Hannàh!" Ettie cried as she reached her and flung her arms around Hannah's waist, pressing her cheek against the wet nightgown. A welter of emotions roiled within Hannah. Love, longing, a feeling of terrible loss. For the first time since she was out of the water, she began to shiver with cold.

"Oh! Oh, Hannah! You're all cold and shivery. Your lips are turning blue. You must be freezing."

Oh, no, thought Hannah, *not freezing, just human.* A sob swelled within her and she thought her heart might break.

ETTIE'S SECRET

NOT FAR FROM THE COVE there was a stand of three birch trees that grew so close together that at the base their trunks fused and offered the perfect V for wedging in a small foot, so it was not too much of a reach to the first branch. Ettie had climbed many times to the first branch but tonight she planned to climb higher. She was going to become a spy and the object of her spying was Hannah.

Since Hannah had returned, Ettie, although relieved and very happy, had sensed that she was distracted. Ettie had thought it would be much better with Lila away. But it was as if Hannah were in another world. Ettie herself had not slept well since Hannah's return and one evening got up to go sit on her favorite window seat to watch the shooting stars. Never had there been so many. She had a small telescope, a gift from her uncle with which she could scan the sky. But on the second night after Hannah had come back, Ettie had caught not a star in the sights of the scope but a figure running across the lawn toward the cove. She knew instantly that it was Hannah. For two more nights from her window Ettie had watched Hannah leave and streak across the lawn to the cove. It was always sometime between midnight and one in the morning. And tonight Ettie planned to be in that tree well before midnight.

Half an hour earlier, Ettie had crept down the back stairs. On the second step from the bottom a tiny glimmering had caught her attention. "What in the world?" she had whispered to herself. At first glance she had thought it might be a paillette from one of her mother's ball gowns. *But Mama wouldn't be going down the back steps in a ball gown.* She had almost laughed out loud at the thought, but had stifled the laugh for if she was found out, there would be masses of trouble.

Now settled fairly high in the tree where she had found a very convenient branch, Ettie examined the little flattened oval she held in the palm of her hand. It was nothing like the trimmings for a ball gown. It was more beautiful, with colors and a luminosity that seemed from another world. *It's Hannah's!*

A cool wind had started to blow in from the sea. Ettie shivered. She should have thought to bring a sweater. *Please, no fog!* Ettie prayed. But the wind was coming from the southeast, the direction that brought thick banks into the bay. *Hurry up, Hannah!*

Half of Ettie's prayers were answered. Hannah came running across the lawn. But the fog had already begun to roll in. She could barely make out Hannah's form now. Her white nightgown was almost indistinguishable from the fog, but her red hair streamed behind her like cooling embers blown from a fire. Two seconds later there was a splash and the embers were quenched. "No!" Ettie moaned.

Ettie was not one to wallow in regret. She had to see more, and began to climb down from the tree. *The fog works both ways*, she thought. *If I can't see her, she can't see me.* And certainly no one from the house could see either of them. The lavender rock was almost awash, but Ettie, shivering, made her way toward it. She had hardly reached the rock when, through the fog, she saw a luminous glow streaking beneath the water's surface. "It's Hannah!" She gripped the iridescent oval in her hand tighter. *This is her secret,* Ettie thought. *And now it is mine. Friends never tell. Never ever!* Clutching the oval, she vowed to never reveal what she knew. "Cross my heart and hope to die," she whispered.

"FOREVER AND EVER?"

"WATCH THIS, HANNAH! Just watch me," Ettie cried out and ducked under the water, poking her stockinged legs straight up into the air. She came up again sputtering. "An underwater handstand! How about that?"

"Wonderful!" Hannah called back.

"I wish you'd come in with me," Ettie said, but then realized what a foolish thing this was to say. But she did often dream that some night, Hannah might take her with her.

Hannah wished she could go into the water as well. But she knew what would happen. It had happened every night since she had returned. Of course now the transformation did not seem mysterious to

Hannah at all. She was accustomed to the feeling of her legs melding together into one powerful tail, her feet merging and then where her ten toes had been, a slight indentation that formed the flukes of the tail.

She had quickly realized that swimming in her nightclothes was ridiculous. She didn't need clothes. She liked the feeling of the water against her bare skin. So she would carefully tuck her clothes away above the high-tide line and slip naked into the water. It was a wonderful, indescribable feeling. Her skin had felt dead before. But naked in the water, every part of her seemed so alive, so profoundly connected with the sea. She felt touched in a way she had never known and that stirred deep feelings within her.

But touch was not the only sense that seemed enhanced when she was in the water. Her hearing became incredibly acute. She could hear the thud of a propeller miles away, the stirring of lobsters in their traps, and she now realized that she could hear human voices, too, even if they were on land. That was why, that first evening, she had heard the cries of

Ettie even though she had been more than a mile from shore.

Slipping out of the household was not a problem, luckily, for both Daze and Susie had their beaux in the village and Florrie had gone back to Boston to prepare the house on Louisburg Square for the Hawleys' return in a few weeks. Hannah went whatever the weather was. There had been a ferocious summer storm when the water of Frenchman Bay churned and turned frothy with whitecaps. Out beyond Egg Rock, the waves from the open sea built into towering mountains of water, and Hannah swam through them, often using her tail to power her into an upward dive into the air above them. If she lofted herself high enough, five or ten feet above the wave, she could flip herself around and dive back toward its crest, sliding down a giant slope of water. She seemed to comprehend the intention of each wave. She could anticipate the precise moment a wave began to curl and when it would collapse entirely in an explosion of spray. It was like being caught in a web of diamonds.

As she watched Ettie now performing water tricks, she thought about a trick she was determined to perfect if only another blow would come through. She had slid down the steep slopes of many offshore waves, but she realized that perhaps the real feat would be to skim across the slopes horizontally, just under the curl of the crest, and try to stay with the wave as long as possible.

Since her return she had found out very little about Lila except that she had been taken away. Hannah had presumed Lila was going to the place she had previously been for the rest treatment. Hannah did not want to question Ettie too much about it. From the other servants, she had learned that the cat had indeed been killed by a rock that Ettie had thrown. Other bits and pieces of the events of that evening leaked out. She wondered in particular about the painter. It had been discovered after the events on the shore that the painting had been defaced. The canvas had been slashed and the face of the girl in the shadows ripped off. When she heard about the destruction of the painting, she knew for certain the painter would never again come to Gladrock, or number 18 in Boston. And not only that, one of the vases had been shattered into hundreds of fragments. And now as Hannah and Ettie walked back up to the house, Hannah could hear the child muttering something through her chattering teeth. "What is that, Ettie? What are you trying to say?"

The child stopped and looked up at Hannah with her clear gray eyes. "Sanatorium."

"What's that?"

"A big, big word."

"What does it mean?"

"You don't know?" Ettie asked. There was a slightly triumphant note in her voice, as if she were somehow pleased that she knew something that an older person didn't.

"I think I might have heard the word." Hannah thought it did sound familiar.

"It's a place where people who have tuberculosis go." Ettie paused. "That's where they took Lila."

"Oh," Hannah said quietly.

They didn't speak until they were back in Ettie's bedroom, where she had changed her clothes and was now sitting in front of her mirror while Hannah combed out her wet hair to braid.

Ettie spoke to their reflections in the mirror. "Of course, Lila doesn't have tuberculosis. But you see, it's much easier to say that than that she's crazy. You go to an asylum if you're crazy. An insane asylum." Ettie went on to explain the finer points of the differences between the two words. "I looked the words up in a dictionary. And it says in the Noah Webster dictionary that an asylum is an institution for the maintenance and care of the blind, the insane, and orphans. You're an orphan, aren't you, Hannah?"

"Yes, but I wasn't in an asylum. I was in The Boston Home for Little Wanderers."

"Oh, that's so sweet sounding." Ettie sighed. "Are you sure there were no blind or insane people there?"

"Yes, quite sure." Hannah was tempted to say that she had never met any insane people until she came to work for the Hawleys. But she resisted. "Just normal children who didn't have any mothers or fathers."

"Who do you think your mother and father were?" Hannah could feel the color drain from her face.

"I . . . I . . ."

"I mean, I think they loved you, Hannah. How could someone not love you? I love you, Hannah." Hannah felt her eyes well with tears.

"Do you now, Ettie?" Ettie looked at her curiously as if to reflect back the hollowness of her words. Hannah felt a twinge of guilt as if she was hoping that Ettie would say no, that she didn't love Hannah, and that then Hannah could break all the ties that bound her to land.

"Yes! But do you love me, Hannah?" Ettie leaned closer to the mirror. The half-finished braid almost slipped through Hannah's hands. Ettie's words did not sound hollow in the least. There was an urgency in her voice. "I mean to say, Hannah, I'm not just your job, am I?"

Hannah's hands froze with the neatly separated bunches of hair twined through her fingers.

"Ettie, what are you saying?" They regarded each other's reflections in the mirror carefully.

"You're paid to scrub the grates, clean the vegetables, and all you do." She paused. "Including braiding my hair . . . but . . . but you do like me, don't you?"

"Of course, Ettie. I like you very much." It sounded so mechanical.

"Of course," Ettie replied softly.

Neither one was now looking at the other in the mirror. They had averted their eyes and for a few seconds Hannah felt as if she had stepped out of her own body and was looking at herself from a slight distance as she continued to braid Ettie's hair.

"Will you promise to stay here forever and ever?"

Hannah looked down at Ettie's face. It looked pinched and nervous. Did Ettie suspect her secret life?

Hannah sighed. "No one can promise forever and ever, Ettie."

"Yes, they can . . . they can . . . Hannah."

"I could promise, Ettie, and I could want to not ever break that promise, but sometimes things can happen that are beyond your control and promises get broken."

"Well, can you promise that if it is in your control, you won't leave?" Ettie looked up at her with her clear gray eyes. Hannah felt a pinch in her heart.

"I can only promise that I'll try," Hannah said.

"You'll try?"

"Yes, I'll try."

Ettie turned around now and, taking Hannah's hand, gave it a ferocious squeeze. *Did my mother try?* Hannah wondered. *Please, God, let her have tried!*

They would be returning to Boston in a very few days. It would be harder for Hannah to go into the sea there. It was farther away for one thing. She could not imagine trekking back and forth between Louisburg Square and the harbor, and what would she wear? Here it was easy to lead a divided life. She could go out in the pitch of a summer night wearing her combis and petticoats. She was hardly ever cold when she walked home. But what would it be like walking through the streets and back alleys of Boston in winter in wet clothes?

It seemed as the last days of summer closed in that Ettie tried more and more to cling to Hannah. Had she seen something on that dreadful yet wonderful night when Hannah had dived into the sea?

Mr. and Mrs. Hawley themselves seemed for the remainder of the summer as shattered as their precious vase. When Hannah had returned that morning, she learned that the painter had left rather abruptly after discovering the ruined portrait.

Stannish Whitman Wheeler had told Hannah, in no uncertain terms, to leave that night, urged her to flee. Had he known somehow what would happen? She had always sensed that he saw things that others did not see, that he could see beneath the surface. He was after all a painter, but that was not the same thing as being able to read the future.

"BEING MER"

STANNISH WHITMAN WHEELER had left Gladrock in a fury. It was understandable; his work had been destroyed. It was his work, however, and not his reputation. A week after the party Perl came into the kitchen for his usual mug of coffee.

"Guess who's back on the island."

"Not Lila, I hope," Mrs. Bletchley said, setting down the mug in front of him.

"No, Mr. Wheeler."

"The painter?" Hannah turned around so quickly that the tea she was drinking slopped over the rim. Her face flushed and the thumping of her heart seemed deafening to her own ears.

"The Stanhopes have engaged him to paint one of

them. Don't know which. And I understand that people be lining up to get him to do their portraits."

Hannah could not quite believe it. She had tried not to allow herself to think about the painter. She had come back, of course, swum back to see him, but when she had heard about the ruined painting, she had given up all hope.

"He's staying over at the inn."

Hannah's mind was in a fever. She had to think of a way to talk to him. A housemaid could not be seen, however, meeting in public with a man of his stature. It was an island after all. The gossip would spread like wildfire. She would have to leave him a note. All morning long as she went about her chores, she composed the note in her head. She was not at all prepared when, just after serving luncheon, Mrs. Bletchley asked if someone would run an errand and go into the village for butter. Nonetheless, Hannah jumped at the chance.

"Just a minute while I change my uniform." Dashing upstairs, she found pen and paper and scrawled a terse message.

Must see you.
Meet me at Seal Point this evening, 11:00
— H

Daze and Florrie and Susie were going for an end-of-summer gathering at the lake. Since the disastrous portrait party, the Hawleys had been retiring early.

Half an hour later Hannah walked through the entrance of the Spruce Inn. A man in a waistcoat and bright green tie approached her. He perceived immediately that she was not a potential guest. "May I help you, miss?"

"Yes, a message for Mr. Wheeler from one of his clients."

"Certainly, miss." He took it crisply and walked it over to the desk. Hannah was quick to leave.

The hours between delivering the note and eleven that night were the longest that Hannah had ever endured. She arrived in the sparse woods of Seal Point an hour early. She dared not swim although this was one of her favorite coves and there was a beautiful ledge where there were seals that she sometimes played with. The ledge was sparkling now in the silvery light of an immense moon.

What would the painter say to her now? What would he do? How could he explain who he was and how he knew . . . knew that she was not quite human? She remembered that on the night of her transformation her first thought as she had lifted her shimmering tail from the water was that she must show the painter. But if he really wasn't one, what would he think? Would he be repulsed? Would he find it disgusting? A sudden panic seized her. She hunched over her knees and, pressing her face into her hands, began to weep.

She was so fraught with her own despair that she did not hear him approach but then felt a touch on her shoulder.

"Why are you crying, Hannah?"

She looked up. His face, though creased with concern, was glorious. "I did go away. I did as you said. I left." She paused. "For the sea."

His shoulders sagged a bit as she said this. He then sat down on the moss-covered forest floor beside her and took her hand.

"Yes, and?"

She looked straight into his eyes, then shook her head wearily. "You know what happened." He pressed her hand to his mouth and kissed it. A deep thrill coursed through her. He was whispering something into her hand. She bent closer to hear the words.

"Why did you come back?" She knew what he meant. Back from the sea, but she needed to hear him say more.

He slipped his arm around her. She leaned her head against his shoulder. "What do you mean 'back'?"

"Back from the sea. Why did you come back?"

"For you," Hannah said simply.

He now took her face in both his hands. His eyes seemed suddenly hard and yet his hands held her face so gently. "Don't you understand?" she asked.

"No, Hannah, you don't understand."

She began to ask what he meant, but the words would simply not come. She was suddenly frightened not of the painter but of what he might say, or was about to say. She raised her own hands to her ears as if to shut out his words, but she couldn't, for his hands still held her face. "Listen to me, Hannah! Right now you can go back and forth, between two worlds. But it will not be this way always. In a year, at the very longest, you must make a choice. You must be of one world or the other."

"No! No!" Hannah was shaking her head now violently.

"Yes, Hannah."

"It's not true."

"It is true. I am living proof. You can never go back!"

Hannah tore herself away and jumped to her feet. "I don't believe you. I just don't." His eyes no longer looked hard, just sad. Terribly sad.

"You must choose your world."

"But it's not fair."

"It has nothing to do with being fair."

"What does it have to do with, then?"

He stood up and looked at her and sighed heavily. "It has to do with being Mer."

By the time Hannah left the point and returned to Gladrock, it was after midnight. She went down to the cove and stood on the lavender rock at its edge. Could it be true, what the painter had said? Why must a choice be made? She looked out on the water. It was a calm night. The lightest of breezes blew, wrinkling the surface into tiny sparkling wavelets. It was as if the moon had broken into a thousand silver pieces. She looked back at the house. She could see a light on in Clarice's room. She was reading late as usual. Ettie's window was dark, but she could picture her softly folded into sleep. *Sweet, sweet, funny little girl. "Am I just your job, Hannah?" — was that how she had put it?* She sighed.

Right now in this moment Hannah felt pressed between two worlds. She had found a place on land. The house was perfect now with Lila gone. She had a position. Daze had told her that when they returned to Boston, she would certainly be promoted to parlor maid. That a new scullery girl would have to be found. This would mean more money. But it wasn't just money. In Boston she could find a way to see the painter. And if, as he said, she had perhaps as long as one year before this choice would have to be made, she could still go into the sea, although how she would manage it in Boston in the winter, she was not sure. Boston was not an island in the middle of the ocean but a port city. Was she greedy to want it all? *But just for now*, she thought. *Just for a little while.*

THE STORM

A HEAVINESS HAD HUNG in the air for several days and erratic gusts of winds slapped the usually calm waters of Frenchman Bay. There was a low boil with spume flying this way and that.

"Hurricane down south, barometer dropping like a shot," Perl announced as he came into the kitchen with a bushel basket of lobsters. " 'T'ain't raining but might as well be. I brought these in 'cause we have to get the dories out of the water and sail *Lark* over to the hole. Think we best secure the buckboards, carts, and traps. Nothing more dangerous than a wheel flying through the air."

"The hole?" Hannah looked up from the peas she was shelling.

"Hurricane hole, safe place for boats during a storm. We'll take her over to that one just by Otter Creek."

"Hurricanes never come here, Perl. They're tropical," Mrs. Bletchley said. "That's why they call them tropical storms." She continued rolling out a piecrust without looking up.

"Maybe, but the fringes of them can skirt us. That's what we got, the outer fringes of this one. She's in the Carolinas now, but telegraph office over at the Revenue Marine station says she's coming up the coast at a steady pace, fifty miles per hour."

"How come they always call hurricanes and storms 'she'?" Susie asked.

"'Cause they're wild, de-ah," Perl retorted with a gruff chuckle.

"Men are wild, too, and I've heard of wicked, wild ones," Daze said with a gleam in her eye.

"Hope you don't go courtin' any of them, daughter," Perl snapped.

Hannah listened to the conversation with interest. She had never thought of storms as he's or she's, but reflected on what Perl said about their wildness. Did she share this wildness, then? She thought about how much she had loved swimming through the storm a few days ago.

All day it was blowy and the servants of Gladrock were busy moving in porch furniture, putting up shutters, and securing the cottage for the major storm that was crashing up the coast. Mrs. Hawley walked around all day long fretting and wringing a handkerchief until it was almost in shreds. "I knew we should have left earlier. I just knew it, Horace. It's insane to stay here this long, through the first week in September. Oh, I wish we were in Paris."

"The last place you would want to be right now is on an ocean liner heading for France, my dear."

"I think it's exciting!" Ettie said. Clarice stuck her nose deeper into the book she was reading. By seven o'clock that evening, telegraph reports came in that the winds had strengthened as the storm made its way up the coast. By midnight it would be ferocious. It was decided that it was much too dangerous for the servants to sleep on the very top floor. The noise on that floor was already deafening and God forbid the roof should be torn off. So soon all the male servants were transporting beds from the third floor to the hallways and corridors of the second floor where the family slept. The female servants were running back and forth with linens. Mrs. Hawley briefly entertained the notion of moving beds to the basement but Mr. Hawley dashed that notion as foolish when he pointed out that there could be storm surge and already there were warnings of coastal flooding.

"Storm surge," Mrs. Hawley repeated with a look of absolute horror, as if the devil incarnate were about to be unleashed in the hallways of Gladrock.

Perl arrived at nine o'clock that evening with the grim news that the hurricane had made its landfall at Cape Rachel, near Portland, with a brutal fury. Forty summer cottages, including the Cape Rachel Yacht Club, and nineteen people had been swept away into the Atlantic. "Oh my God!" Mrs. Hawley gave a little yelp and collapsed on a sofa.

By now the rain was pouring down in slanting sheets blown almost horizontal by the wind. Inside, the noise was a fearsome cacophony of creaks and moans as shutters clattered on their hinges, shingles flew from the roof, and the stately trees creaked in despair at the wrathful winds slamming across the lawn. Then suddenly there was a tremendous crash and the whole house shook.

"What's that?" Clarice cried out. Horace Hawley and Mr. Marston looked at each other. "It must be the grand oak," Mr. Hawley said.

"I'm afraid you might be right, sir," the butler replied.

But while everyone was trembling with fear as the eye of the hurricane approached, Hannah was fraught with anticipation. She tried to imagine the bay, especially the seas off Egg Rock — towering waves crashing, spume flying, immense surges swelling all around her. She prayed that everyone would fall asleep, and soon, so she could steal out. She knew that the worst dangers would be those on land — falling trees, the wheels of wagons careening on gusts of wind — but if she could get to the water, she would be safe.

They were all, servants and family alike, now huddled together in the large drawing room. Mrs. Bletchley had made a kettle of cocoa and Susie and Daze and Hannah had prepared four platters of sandwiches. Mr. Hawley stood up and walked to one of the many barometers in the house. He summoned Perl and Mr. Marston.

"Look here. She's dropping like a shot. Hit twenty-eight and now the mercury's going to twenty-seven. I don't believe I've ever seen the atmospheric pressure this low."

Perl yawned. "Makes you sleepy when she gets that low. The eye must be near."

So, thought Hannah. *Not only are storms and hurricanes female but mercury and pressure are.* She was not quite sure what he meant by atmospheric pressure. Hannah noticed that suddenly everyone appeared to be rather lethargic. Perl was not the only one yawning.

"Well, I think we should turn in," Mr. Hawley said. "Perl, Marston's and your cots are near our door. If there is anything untoward, don't hesitate one minute to come in."

"A-yuh," replied Pearl.

"Certainly, sir," said Marston.

Hannah was not one bit sleepy. If anything, she had never felt more alive as the atmospheric pressure continued to plummet and the mercury slid down to almost twenty-seven inches in the barometer. On one side of her in the hallway Daze slept, on the other, Susie. Hannah slipped from the bed, made her way downstairs to the kitchen, and stepped outside.

She stood for a moment on the pantry porch, clinging to the post. It was an amazing night. The grand oak had been uprooted and fallen on the porch, crashing through its roof. She saw random boards, most likely from the outbuildings, tool sheds, stables, and greenhouses, flying through the air. Hannah immediately knew that if she tried to run across this wind, there was no way she would make it to the water. She would be picked up by a gust and smashed against a tree or a building. But if she crawled on her belly, she would offer less of a target. She sat down on the steps and scooted on her bottom down to the path, then turned onto her stomach and began slithering across the lawn. Now the only thing she feared was something falling upon her. She was nearly half-way across the grass when she heard a clacking and squawking above her. She covered her head and looked up.

"Good God in heaven," she muttered. It was a chicken coop complete with chickens flying through the air. It crash-landed a few yards from her. Momentarily stunned, the chickens stopped their squawking, then erupted again in a mad clucking. One of them managed to walk from the coop but in another second it was picked up by the wind and was soon tumbling head over tail through the air. Feathers blew down into the grass just in front of Hannah as she continued her crawl toward the sea. In the path, a large birch had been torn up but she managed to get around it. She saw the bodies of some tiny baby birds flung from their nest.

She was almost to the cove when suddenly the sea came to her. A surge of waves like immense watery hands plucked her from the lawn, from the grass, from the crashed chicken coops and uprooted trees, and bore her into the water.

She felt the wonderful familiar tingle in her legs as they fused together, the power and strength of that glistening tail. With one flick she propelled herself into the deeper water. She kept swimming down beneath the churnings and the surface rage of the bay. She felt the drag of the undercurrents, but they only made the swimming more interesting. It was as if she were trying to thread her way through a water maze. She wanted to get out to beyond Egg Rock where the really big waves would be crashing. In calm weather it took her only two rises to break through the surface for air. But in this hurricane she might have to take three. It was on her second rise that she noticed that everything around her had grown incredibly still. She swam now so that she was almost in a vertical position and lifted herself higher out of the water, which she could do easily by treading water with the flukes of her tail. She seemed to be in a windless pocket of the sea. The water was smooth. When she looked around she saw a swirling vapor, but when she tipped her head straight, it was clear — only stars. *This must be the eye of the hurricane*, she thought. *I am finally at peace.* Then she laughed. *At peace in the eye of a storm!* It seemed as if she had traveled vast distances to discover something at the very center of her being that she had always known.

And yet, she thought as she swirled herself about in the still water to face the coast that was only a dim scratchy line behind a veil of flying froth and spume, *and yet all that I have known of love is there.* She could almost hear Ettie's voice and feel the painter's eyes on her. She realized with instant clarity that she did not really know what awaited her.

But suddenly she sensed a presence. It was nearby. It wasn't a seal. She knew how seals swam, she knew their scent. Her heart began to beat wildly. There was someone near . . . someone. . . . She looked about, frantic with excitement. There was no fear, only the joy of sensing another. The clouds and rains were scraped away and a stream of moonlight fell upon the calm lake in the middle of the stormy sea. There was a glistening flash as the moon's silver light illuminated a tail, a tail just like her own.

I am not alone! There is a world out there.